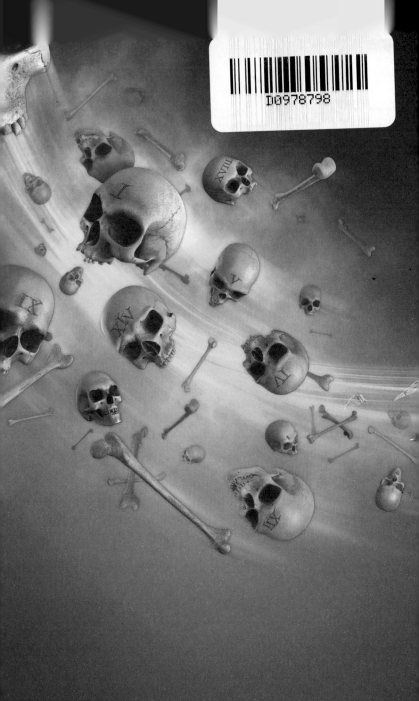

YOU HAVE BEEN CHOSEN AS
THE MOST LIKELY TO SUCCEED
IN THE GREATEST, MOST PERILOUS
UNDERTAKING OF ALL TIME –
A QUEST OF VITAL IMPORTANCE
TO THE CAHILL FAMILY
AND THE WORLD AT LARGE....

THE MAZE OF BONES

WITHDRAWN

RICK RIORDAN

SCHOLASTIC INC.

NEW YORK TORONTO LONDON AUCKLAND SYDNEY
MEXICO CITY NEW DELHI HONG KONG BUENOS AIRES

www.NessieLives.com

Library of Congress Control Number: 2007938689

ISBN-13: 978-0-545-09054-4

10 9 8   13

Book design and illustration by SJI Associates, Inc.

Library edition, September 2008

Printed in China 62

Scholastic US: 557 Broadway • New York, NY 10012
Scholastic Canada: 604 King Street West • Toronto, ON M5V 1E1
Scholastic New Zealand Limited: Private Bag 94407 • Greenmount, Manukau 2141
Scholastic UK Ltd.: Euston House • 24 Eversholt Street • London NW1 1DB

To Haley and Patrick,
who accepted the challenge

CHAPTER 1

Five minutes before she died, Grace Cahill changed her will.

Her lawyer brought out the alternate version, which had been her most guarded secret for seven years. Whether or not she would actually be crazy enough to use it, William McIntyre had never been certain.

"Madam," he asked, "are you sure?"

Grace gazed out the window, across the sunlit meadows of her estate. Her cat, Saladin, snuggled beside her as he had throughout her illness, but his presence was not enough to comfort her today. She was about to set in motion events that might cause the end of civilization.

"Yes, William." Her every breath was painful. "I'm sure."

William broke the seal on the brown leather folder. He was a tall craggy man. His nose was pointed like a sundial so it always cast a shadow over one side of his face. He had been Grace's adviser, her closest confidant, for half her life. They'd shared many secrets over the years, but none as perilous as this.

He held the document for her to review. A fit of coughing wracked her body. Saladin meowed with concern. Once the coughing passed, William helped her take the pen. She scrawled her weak signature across the paper.

"They're so young," William lamented. "If only their parents—"

"But their parents didn't," Grace said bitterly. "And now the children must be old enough. They are our only chance."

"If they don't succeed—"

"Then five hundred years of work have been for nothing," Grace said. "Everything collapses. The family, the world—all of it."

William nodded grimly. He took the folder from her hands.

Grace sat back, stroking Saladin's silver fur. The scene outside the window made her sad. It was too gorgeous a day to die. She wanted to have one last picnic with the children. She wanted to be young and strong and travel the world again.

But her eyesight was failing. Her lungs labored. She clutched her jade necklace—a good-luck talisman she'd found in China years ago. It had seen her through many close calls with death, many lucky misses. But the talisman couldn't help her anymore.

She'd worked hard to prepare for this day. Still, there was so much she'd left undone . . . so much she had never told the children.

"It will have to be enough," she whispered.

And with that, Grace Cahill closed her eyes for the last time.

When he was sure Grace had passed away, William McIntyre went to the window and closed the curtains. William preferred darkness. It seemed more proper for the business at hand.

The door opened behind him. Grace's cat hissed and disappeared under the bed.

William didn't look back. He was staring at Grace Cahill's signature on her new will, which had just become the most important document in the Cahill family's history.

"Well?" a brusque voice said.

William turned. A man stood in the doorway, his face obscured by shadows, his suit as black as oil.

"It's time," William said. "Make sure they suspect nothing."

William couldn't tell for sure, but he thought the man in black smiled.

"Don't worry," the man promised. "They'll never have a clue."

CHAPTER 2

Dan Cahill thought he had the most annoying big sister on the planet. And that was *before* she set fire to two million dollars.

It all started when they went to their grandmother's funeral. Secretly, Dan was excited, because he was hoping to make a rubbing of the tombstone after everyone else was gone. He figured Grace wouldn't care. She'd been a cool grandmother.

Dan loved collecting things. He collected baseball cards, autographs of famous outlaws, Civil War weapons, rare coins, and every cast he'd ever had since kindergarten (all twelve of them). At the moment, what he liked collecting best were charcoal rubbings of tombstones. He had some awesome ones back at the apartment. His favorite read:

PRUELLA GOODE
1891–1929
I'M DEAD. LET'S HAVE A PARTY.

He figured if he had a rubbing of Grace's tombstone in his collection, maybe it wouldn't feel quite so much like she was gone forever.

Anyway, the whole way from Boston to the funeral in Bristol County, his great-aunt Beatrice was driving like a very slow lunatic. She went twenty-five miles an hour on the highway and kept drifting across lanes so the other cars honked and swerved and ran into guardrails and stuff. Aunt Beatrice just kept clutching the wheel with her jeweled fingers. Her wrinkly face was made up with Day-Glo red lipstick and rouge, which made her blue hair look even bluer. Dan wondered if she gave the other drivers nightmares about old clowns.

"Amy!" she snapped, as another SUV careened down the exit ramp because Beatrice had just pulled in front of it. "Stop reading in the car! It's not safe!"

"But, Aunt Beatrice—"

"Young lady, close that book!"

Amy did, which was typical. She never put up a fight with adults. Amy had long reddish-brown hair, unlike Dan's, which was dark blond. This helped Dan pretend his sister was an alien imposter, but unfortunately they had the same eyes—green like jade, their grandmother used to say.

Amy was three years older and six inches taller than Dan, and she never let him forget it—like being fourteen was such a big deal. Usually, she wore jeans and some old T-shirt because she didn't like people noticing her, but today she was wearing a black dress so she looked like a vampire's bride.

Dan hoped her outfit was as uncomfortable as his stupid suit and tie. Aunt Beatrice had thrown a fit when he tried to go to the funeral in his ninja clothes. It wasn't as if Grace would care if he was comfortable and deadly, the way he felt when he pretended to be a ninja, but of course Aunt Beatrice didn't understand. Sometimes it was hard for him to believe she and Grace were sisters.

"Remind me to fire your au pair as soon as we return to Boston," Beatrice grumbled. "You two have been entirely too spoiled."

"Nellie's nice!" Dan protested.

"Hmph! This *Nellie* almost let you burn down the neighbor's apartment building!"

"Exactly!"

Every couple of weeks, Beatrice fired their au pair and hired a new one. The only good thing was that Aunt Beatrice didn't live with them personally. She lived across town in a building that didn't allow kids, so sometimes it took her a few days to hear about Dan's latest exploits.

Nellie had lasted longer than most. Dan liked her because she made amazing waffles and she usually cranked her iPod up to brain-damage level. She didn't even hear when Dan's bottle rocket collection went off and strafed the building across the alley. Dan would miss Nellie when she got fired.

Aunt Beatrice kept driving and muttering about spoiled children. Amy secretly went back to her huge book. The last two days, since they got the news about Grace's death, Amy had been reading even more than usual. Dan knew it was her way of hiding, but he kind of resented it because it shut him out, too.

"What are you reading this time?" he asked. "*Medieval European Doorknobs*? *Bath Towels Through the Ages*?"

Amy gave him an ugly face—or an uglier-than-usual face. "None of your business, dweeb."

"You can't call a ninja lord *dweeb*. You have disgraced the family. You must commit seppuku."

Amy rolled her eyes.

After a few more miles, the city melted into farmland. It started to look like Grace country, and even though Dan had promised himself he wouldn't get sappy, he began to feel sad. Grace had been the coolest ever. She'd treated him and Amy like real people, not kids. That's why she'd insisted they simply call her Grace, not Grandmother or Gran or Nana or any silly name like that. She'd been one of the only people who'd ever cared about them. Now she was dead, and they had to go to the funeral and see a bunch of relatives who had *never* been nice to them. . . .

The family cemetery sat at the bottom of the hill from the mansion. Dan thought it was kind of stupid they'd hired a hearse to carry Grace a hundred yards down the driveway. They could've put wheels on the coffin like they have on suitcases and that would've worked just as well.

Summer storm clouds rumbled overhead. The family mansion looked dark and gloomy on its hill, like a lord's castle. Dan loved the place, with its billion rooms and chimneys and stained glass windows.

He loved the family graveyard even more. A dozen crumbling tombstones spread out across a green meadow ringed in trees, right next to a little creek. Some of the stones were so old the writing had faded away. Grace used to take Amy and him down to the meadow on their weekend visits. Grace and Amy would spend the afternoon on a picnic blanket, reading and talking, while Dan explored the graves and the woods and the creek.

Stop that, Dan told himself. *You're getting sentimental.*

"So many people," Amy murmured, as they walked down the driveway.

"You're not going to freak out, are you?"

Amy fiddled with the collar of her dress. "I'm—I'm not freaking out. I just—"

"You hate crowds," he finished. "But you *knew* there'd be a crowd. They come every year."

Each winter, as long as Dan could remember, Grace had invited relatives from all over the world for a weeklong holiday. The mansion filled up with Chinese Cahills and British Cahills and South African Cahills and Venezuelan Cahills. Most of them didn't even go by the name Cahill, but Grace assured him they were all related. She'd explain about cousins and second cousins and cousins three times removed until Dan's brain started to hurt. Amy would usually go hide in the library with the cat.

"I know," she said. "But . . . I mean, *look* at them all."

She had a point. About four hundred people were gathering at the grave site.

"They just want her fortune," Dan decided.

"Dan!"

"Well? It's true."

They had just joined the procession when Dan suddenly got flipped upside down.

"Hey!" he yelled.

"Look, guys," a girl said. "We caught a rat!"

Dan wasn't in a good position to see, but he could make out the Holt sisters—Madison and Reagan—standing on either side of him, holding him by his ankles. The twins had matching purple running suits, blond pigtails, and crooked smiles. They were only eleven, same as Dan, but they had no trouble holding him. Dan saw more purple running suits behind them—the rest of the Holt family. Their pit bull,

Arnold, raced around their legs and barked.

"Let's fling him into the creek," Madison said.

"I wanna fling him into the bushes!" Reagan said. "We never do *my* ideas!"

Their older brother, Hamilton, laughed like an idiot. Next to him, their dad, Eisenhower Holt, and their mom, Mary-Todd, grinned like this was all good fun.

"Now, girls," Eisenhower said. "We can't go flinging people at a funeral. This is a happy occasion!"

"Amy!" Dan called. "A little help here?"

Her face had gone pale. She mumbled, "Dr-dr-drop . . ."

Dan sighed in exasperation. "She's trying to say 'DROP ME!'"

Madison and Reagan did—on his head.

"Ow!" Dan said.

"M-M-Madison!" Amy protested.

"Y-y-yes?" Madison mimicked. "I think all those books are turning your brain to mush, weirdo."

If it had been anybody else, Dan would've hit back, but he knew better with the Holts. Even Madison and Reagan, the youngest, could cream him. The whole Holt family was way too buff. They had meaty hands and thick necks and faces that looked like G.I. Joe figures. Even the mom looked like she should be shaving and chewing on a cigar.

"I hope you losers took a good last look around the house," Madison said. "You're not going to be invited back here anymore, now that the old witch is dead."

"Rawf!" said Arnold the pit bull.

Dan looked around for Beatrice, but as usual she wasn't anywhere near them. She'd drifted off to talk to the other old people.

"Grace wasn't a witch," Dan said. "And *we're* going to inherit this place!"

The big brother, Hamilton, laughed. "Yeah, right." His hair was combed toward the middle so it stuck up like a shark fin. "Wait till they read the will, runt. I'm gonna kick you out myself!"

"All right, team," the dad said. "Enough of this. Formation!"

The family lined up and started jogging toward the grave site, knocking other relatives out of their way as Arnold snapped at everyone's heels.

"Is your head okay?" Amy asked guiltily.

Dan nodded. He was a little annoyed Amy hadn't helped him, but there was no point complaining about it. She always got tongue-tied around other people. "Man, I hate the Holts."

"We've got worse problems." Amy pointed toward the grave site, and Dan's heart sank.

"The Cobras," he muttered.

Ian and Natalie Kabra were standing by Grace's coffin, looking like perfect little angels as they talked to the preacher. They wore matching designer mourning outfits that complemented their silky black hair and cinnamon-colored skin. They could've been child supermodels.

"They won't try anything during the funeral," Dan said hopefully. "They're just here for Grace's money like the rest of them. But they won't get it."

Amy frowned. "Dan . . . did you really believe what you said, about us inheriting the mansion?"

"Of course! You know Grace liked us best. We spent more time with her than anybody."

Amy sighed like Dan was too young to understand, which Dan hated.

"Come on," she said. "We might as well get this over with." And together they waded into the crowd.

The funeral was a blur to Dan. The minister said some stuff about ashes. They lowered the coffin into the ground. Everybody tossed in a shovelful of dirt. Dan thought the mourners enjoyed this part too much, especially Ian and Natalie.

He recognized a few more relatives: Alistair Oh, the old Korean dude with the diamond-tipped walking stick who always insisted they call him Uncle; the Russian lady Irina Spasky, who had a twitch in one eye so everybody called her Blinky behind her back; the Starling triplets — Ned, Ted, and Sinead, who looked like part of a cloned Ivy League lacrosse team. Even that kid from television was there: Jonah Wizard. He stood to one side, getting his picture taken with a bunch of girls, and there was a line of people waiting to talk to him. He was dressed just like on TV, with lots of silver chains and bracelets, ripped jeans, and a black muscle shirt (which was kind of stupid, since he didn't have any muscles). An older African-American guy in a business suit stood behind him, punching notes in a BlackBerry. Probably Jonah's dad. Dan had heard that Jonah Wizard was related to the Cahills, but he'd never seen him in person before. He wondered if he should get an autograph for his collection.

After the service, a guy in a charcoal-gray suit stepped to the podium. He looked vaguely familiar to Dan. The man had a long pointed nose and a balding head. He reminded Dan of a vulture.

"Thank you all for coming," he said gravely. "I am William McIntyre, Madame Cahill's lawyer and executor."

"Executor?" Dan whispered to Amy. "He killed her?"

"No, you idiot," Amy whispered back. "That means he's in charge of her will."

"If you will look inside your programs," William McIntyre continued, "some of you will find a gold invitation card."

Excited murmuring broke out as four hundred people leafed through their programs. Then most of them cursed and shouted complaints when they found nothing. Dan ripped through his program. Inside was a card with a gold-leafed border. It read:

Dan and Amy Cahill are hereby invited to the
reading of
the last will and testament of Grace Cahill.

WHERE
The Great Hall, Cahill Manor

WHEN
Now

"I knew it!" Dan said.

"I assure you," Mr. McIntyre said, raising his voice above the crowd, "the invitations were not done randomly. I apologize to those of you who were excluded. Grace Cahill meant you no disrespect. Of all the members of the Cahill clan, only a few were chosen as the most likely."

The crowd started yelling and arguing. Finally, Dan couldn't stand it anymore. He called out, "Most likely to what?"

"In your case, Dan," Ian Kabra muttered right behind him, "to be a stupid American git."

His sister, Natalie, giggled. She was holding an invitation and looking very pleased with herself.

Before Dan could kick Ian in a soft spot, the gray-suited man answered. "To be the beneficiaries of Grace Cahill's will. Now, if you please, those with invitations will gather in the Great Hall."

People with invitations hurried toward the house like somebody had just yelled "Free food!"

Natalie Kabra winked at Dan. "*Ciao,* cousin. Must run collect our fortune." Then she and her brother strolled up the drive.

"Forget them," Amy said. "Dan, maybe you're right. Maybe we'll inherit something."

But Dan frowned. If this invitation was such a great thing, why did the lawyer guy look so grim? And why had Grace included the Kabras?

As he passed through the main entrance of the mansion, Dan glanced up at the stone crest above the door—a large C surrounded by four smaller designs— a dragon, a bear, a wolf, and two snakes entwined around a sword. The crest had always fascinated Dan, though he didn't know what it meant. All the animals seemed to glare at him, like they were about to strike. He followed the crowd inside, wondering why those animals were so mad.

The Great Hall was as big as a basketball court, with tons of armor and swords lining the walls and huge windows that looked like Batman could crash through them any minute.

William McIntyre stood at a table in front with a projector screen behind him, while everybody else filed into rows of seats. There were about forty people in all, including the Holts and the Kabras and Aunt Beatrice, who looked completely disgusted to be there — or maybe she was just disgusted that every-body *else* had been invited to her sister's will reading.

Mr. McIntyre raised his hand for quiet. He slipped a document from a brown leather folder, adjusted his bifocals, and began to read: "'I, Grace Cahill, being of sound mind and body, do hereby divide my entire estate among those who accept the challenge and those who do not.'"

"Whoa," Eisenhower Holt interrupted. "What challenge? What's she mean?"

"I am getting to that, sir." Mr. McIntyre cleared his throat and continued: "'You have been chosen as the most likely to succeed in the greatest, most perilous undertaking of all time — a quest of vital importance to the Cahill family and the world at large.'"

Forty people started talking at once, asking questions and demanding answers.

"'Perilous undertaking'?" Cousin Ingrid shouted. "What is she talking about?"

"I thought this was about money!" Uncle José yelled. "A quest? Who does she think we are? We're Cahills, not adventurers!"

Dan noticed Ian and Natalie Kabra exchange a meaningful look. Irina Spasky whispered something in Alistair Oh's ear, but most of the other spectators looked as confused as Dan felt.

"Ladies and gentlemen, please," Mr. McIntyre said. "If you will direct your attention to the screen, perhaps Madame Cahill can explain things better than I."

Dan's heart did a flip-flop. What was Mr. McIntyre talking about? Then a projector on the ceiling hummed to life. The shouting in the room died down as Grace's image flickered on the screen.

She was sitting up in bed with Saladin on her lap. She wore a black dressing gown, like she was a mourner at her own funeral, but she looked healthier than the last time Dan had seen her. Her complexion was pink. Her face and hands didn't look as thin. The video must've been made months ago, before her cancer got bad. Dan got a lump in his throat. He had a crazy urge to call to her: *Grace, it's me! It's Dan!* But of course it was just an image. He looked at Amy and saw a tear trickling down the base of her nose.

"Fellow Cahills," Grace said. "If you are watching this, it means I am dead, and I have decided to use my alternate will. No doubt you are arguing amongst yourselves and giving poor Mr. McIntyre a hard time about this contest I have instituted." Grace gave the camera a dry smile. "You always were a stubborn bunch. For once, close your mouths and listen."

"Hey, wait a minute!" Eisenhower Holt protested, but his wife shushed him.

"I assure you," Grace continued, "this contest is no trick. It is deadly serious business. Most of you know you belong to the Cahill family, but many of you may not realize just how important our family is. I tell you the Cahills have had a greater impact on human civilization than any other family in history."

More confused shouting broke out. Irina Spasky stood up and yelled, "Silence! I wish to hear!"

"My relatives," Grace's image said, "you stand on the brink of our greatest challenge. Each of you has the potential to succeed. Some of you may decide to form a team with other people in this room to pursue the challenge. Some of you may prefer to take up the challenge alone. Most of you, I'm afraid, will decline the challenge and run away with your tails between your legs. Only *one* team will succeed, and each of you must sacrifice your share of the inheritance to participate."

She held up a manila envelope sealed with red wax. Her eyes were as bright and hard as steel. "If you accept, you shall be given the first of thirty-nine clues. These clues will lead you to a secret, which, should you find it, will make you the most powerful, influential human beings on the planet. You will realize the destiny of the Cahill family. I now beg you all to listen to Mr. McIntyre. Allow him to explain the rules. Think long and hard before you make your choice." She stared straight into the camera, and Dan wanted her to say something special to them: *Dan and Amy, I'll miss you most of all. Nobody else in this room really matters to me.* Something like that.

Instead, Grace said, "I'm counting on you all. Good luck, and good-bye."

The screen went dark. Amy gripped Dan's hand. Her fingers were trembling. To Dan, it felt like they'd just lost Grace all over again. Then everyone around them started talking at once.

"Greatest family in history?" Cousin Ingrid yelled. "Is she crazy?"

"Stubborn?" Eisenhower Holt shouted. "She called *us* stubborn?"

"William!" Alistair Oh's voice rose above the rest. "Just a moment! There are people here I don't even recognize, people who may not even be members of the family. How do we know—"

"If you are in this room, sir," Mr. McIntyre said, "you are a Cahill. Whether your surname is Cahill or not doesn't matter. Everyone here has Cahill blood."

"Even you, Mr. McIntyre?" Natalie Kabra asked in her silky British accent.

The old lawyer flushed. "That, miss, is beside the point. Now, if I might be allowed to finish—"

"But what's this about sacrificing our inheritance?" Aunt Beatrice complained. "Where's the money? It's just like my sister to come up with some foolishness!"

"Madam," Mr. McIntyre said, "you may certainly decline the challenge. If you do, you will receive what is under your chair."

Immediately, forty people felt around under their chairs. Eisenhower Holt was so anxious he picked up Reagan's chair with her still in it. Dan discovered an envelope under his, stuck on with tape. When he opened it, he found a green slip of paper with a bunch of numbers and the words ROYAL BANK OF SCOTLAND. Amy had one, too. So did everybody in the room.

"What you now hold is a bank voucher," Mr. McIntyre explained. "It shall only be activated if and when you renounce your claim to the challenge. If you so choose, each of you may walk out of this room with one million dollars and never have to think of Grace Cahill or her last wishes again. Or . . . you may choose a clue—a single clue that will be your only inheritance. No money. No property. Just a clue that might lead you to the most important treasure in the world and make you powerful beyond belief . . ."

William's gray eyes seemed to settle on Dan particularly. ". . . or it might kill you. One million dollars or the clue. You have five minutes to decide."

CHAPTER 3

Amy Cahill thought she had the most annoying little brother on the planet. And that was *before* he almost got her killed.

It all started when Mr. McIntyre read their grandmother's will and showed them the video.

Amy sat there in shock. She found herself holding a green slip of paper worth one million dollars. A challenge? A dangerous secret? What was going on? She stared at the blank projector screen. She couldn't believe her grandmother would do something like this. The video must have been made months ago, judging from the way Grace had looked. Seeing her on the screen like that had stung Amy worse than salt in a cut. How could Grace have been planning something this huge and not have warned them in advance?

Amy never expected to inherit much. All she wanted was something to remember Grace by—a keepsake, maybe one piece of her beautiful jewelry. Now this . . . she felt completely lost.

It didn't help that Dan was jumping around like he needed to go to the restroom. "One million dollars!" he squealed. "I could get a Mickey Mantle rookie card *and* a Babe Ruth 1914!"

His tie was crooked, which matched his crooked grin. He had a scar under one eye from when he'd gone commando-raiding at seven and fallen on his plastic AK-47. That's just the kind of little demon he was. But what Amy really resented was how comfortable he seemed, like all these people didn't bother him.

Amy hated crowds. She felt like everyone was watching her, waiting for her to make a fool of herself. Sometimes in her nightmares, she dreamed she was at the bottom of a pit, and all the people she knew were staring down at her, laughing. She'd try to climb out of the pit, but she could never make it.

Right now, all she wanted to do was run up to Grace's library, close the door, and curl up with a book. She wanted to find Saladin, Grace's Egyptian Mau, and cuddle with him. But Grace was dead, and the poor cat . . . who knew where he was now? She blinked tears out of her eyes, thinking about the last time she'd seen her grandmother.

You will make me proud, Amy, Grace had said. They'd been sitting on Grace's big four-poster bed, with Saladin purring next to them. Grace had shown her a hand-drawn map of Africa and told her stories about the adventures she'd had when she was a young explorer. Grace had looked thin and frail, but the fire in her eyes was as fierce as ever. The sunlight turned her hair to pure silver. *I had many adventures, my dear, but they will pale next to yours.*

Amy wanted to cry. How could Grace think that Amy would have great adventures? She could barely muster enough courage to go to school every morning.

"I could get a ninja sword," Dan kept babbling. "Or a Civil War saber!"

"Dan, shut up," she said. "This is serious."

"But the money—"

"I know," she said. "But if we took the money, we'd need to keep it for college and stuff. You know how Aunt Beatrice is."

Dan frowned like he'd forgotten. He knew good and well that Aunt Beatrice only looked after them for Grace's sake. Amy always wished Grace had adopted them after their parents died, but she hadn't. For reasons she never explained, she'd pressured Beatrice into being their guardian instead.

For the last seven years, Dan and Amy had been at Beatrice's mercy, living in a tiny little apartment with a series of au pairs. Beatrice paid for everything, but she didn't pay much. Amy and Dan got enough to eat and a new set of clothes every six months, but that was it. No birthday presents. No special treats. No allowance. They went to regular public school and Amy never had extra money to buy books. She used the public library, or sometimes she'd hang out at the second-hand bookshop on Boylston, where the staff knew her. Dan made a little money on his own trading collectible cards, but it wasn't much.

Every weekday for seven years, Amy had resented Grace for not raising them herself, but every weekend Amy just couldn't stay mad at her. When they came to the mansion, Grace gave them undivided attention. She treated them like the most important people in the world. Whenever Amy got up the courage to ask why they couldn't stay with Grace all the time, Grace just smiled sadly. *There are reasons, dear. Someday, you will understand.*

Now Grace was gone. Amy didn't know what Aunt Beatrice would do, but they could definitely use money. It would mean they'd have some independence. They could get a bigger apartment, maybe. They could buy books whenever they wanted and even go to college. Amy was desperate to go to Harvard. She wanted to study history and archaeology. Her mom would've liked that.

At least . . . Amy hoped she would have. Amy knew so little about her parents. She didn't even know why she and Dan carried their mom's maiden name—Cahill—when their dad's last name had been Trent. She'd asked Grace about it once, but Grace had only smiled. "It's how your parents wanted it," she said. But the stubborn pride in her voice made Amy wonder if it had really been Grace's idea for them to carry the Cahill name.

Amy had trouble remembering her mother's face, or *anything* about her parents before the terrible night they died. And that was something Amy tried hard not to think about.

"Okay," Dan said slowly. "So I'll spend *my* million on my collection. You can spend yours on college. And everybody's happy."

Amy felt heartsick. Arguments were breaking out all over the room. The Holts looked like they were conducting a combat exercise. Sinead Starling was holding her brothers, Ned and Ted, apart so they wouldn't strangle each other. Irina Spasky was talking in rapid-fire Russian to that kid from the reality TV show, Jonah Wizard, and his dad, but from the way they were staring back at her, it was obvious they didn't speak Russian. Angry voices filled the Great Hall. It was like they were tearing up Grace bit by bit, squabbling over her inheritance. They didn't care at all that Amy's grandmother had just passed away.

Then somebody right behind her said, "You'll decline the challenge, of course."

It was Ian Kabra, with his annoying sister, Natalie, at his side. Despite herself, Amy's stomach did a little somersault, because Ian was very good-looking. He had gorgeous dark skin, amber eyes, and a perfect smile. He was fourteen, same as her, but he dressed like a grown-up, in a silk suit and tie. He even smelled good, like clove. Amy hated herself for noticing.

"I would be sad if something happened to you," Ian purred. "And you so need the money."

Natalie put her hands to her mouth in mock surprise. She looked like a life-size doll in her satin dress, her luxurious black hair swept over one shoulder. "That's right, Ian! They're poor. I keep forgetting. It seems so odd we're related, doesn't it?"

Amy felt herself blush. She wanted to say something scathing in reply, but her voice wouldn't work.

"Oh, yeah?" Dan said. "Well, maybe we're *not* related! Maybe you're mutant aliens, because *real* kids don't dress like bankers and fly around in their daddy's private jet."

Ian smiled. "You misunderstand me, dear cousin. We're very happy for you. We want you to take the money, have a wonderful life, and never think about us again."

"G-G-Grace," Amy managed, hating that her voice wouldn't cooperate. "G-Grace would want—"

"Would want you to risk your lives?" Ian supplied. "How do you know? Did she tell you about this contest she was planning?"

Neither Amy nor Dan answered.

"I see," Ian said. "That must be terrible—thinking you were Grace's favorites and then being left in the dark like that. Perhaps you weren't as important to the old woman as you thought, eh?"

"Now, Ian," Natalie chided. "Perhaps Grace just knew they weren't up to the challenge. It sounds quite dangerous." Natalie smiled at Amy. "We'd hate to see you suffer a painful death, wouldn't we? Ta-ta!"

The Kabras drifted off through the crowd.

"*Ta-ta*," Dan mimicked. "What losers."

Part of Amy wanted to chase down the Kabras and hit them with a chair. But part of her wanted to crawl under a rock and hide. She'd wanted so badly to tell them off, but she hadn't even been able to *speak*.

"They're taking the challenge," she muttered.

"Well, duh!" Dan said. "What's another two million dollars to them? They can afford to give it up."

"They were threatening us. They don't want us involved."

"Maybe *they'll* suffer a painful death," Dan mused. "I wonder what the treasure is, anyway."

"Does it matter?" Amy asked bitterly. "*We* can't look for it. We barely have enough money for bus passes."

But still she found herself wondering. Grace had explored all over the world. Could the treasure be a lost Egyptian tomb . . . or pirates' gold? Mr. McIntyre had said the prize would make the winners the most powerful human beings on earth. What could do that? And why were there exactly thirty-nine clues?

She couldn't help being curious. She loved mysteries. When she was younger, she used to pretend her mother was still alive, and they would travel together to archaeological digs. Sometimes Grace would go, too, just the three of them together, happily exploring the world, but that was just silly pretending.

"Too bad," Dan grumbled, "I'd love to wipe the smiles off the Cobras' faces. . . ."

Just then, Aunt Beatrice grabbed their arms. Her face was contorted with rage and her breath smelled like mothballs. "You two will do nothing ridiculous! I fully intend to take my million dollars, and you will do the same! Never fear, I'll put it in an account for you until you're adults. I'll only spend the interest. In return, I will allow you to continue as my wards."

Amy choked with rage. "You . . . you'll *allow* us to be your wards? You'll *allow* us to give you our two million dollars?"

As soon as she said it, she couldn't believe she'd managed to get the words out. Beatrice usually scared her to death. Even Dan looked impressed.

"Watch your place, young lady!" Beatrice warned. "Do the responsible thing or else!"

"Or else what?" Dan asked innocently.

Beatrice's face turned bright red. "Or else, you little upstart, I will disown you and leave you to Social Services. You will be penniless orphans, and I'll make sure no Cahill ever helps you again! This whole business is absurd. You'll take the money and wash your hands of my sister's ridiculous scheme for finding the—"

She stopped abruptly.

"Finding the what?" Dan asked.

"Never you mind," Beatrice said. With a shock, Amy realized Aunt Beatrice was *scared*. "Just make the right choice, or you will never have my support again!"

She marched off. Amy looked at Dan, but before she could say anything, Mr. McIntyre rang a little bell. Slowly, the wrangling and arguing in the Great Hall died down. The assembly took their seats.

"It is time," Mr. McIntyre said. "I must warn you that once the choice is made, there is no turning back. No changing minds."

"Wait a moment, William," Alistair Oh said. "This isn't fair. We know almost nothing about the challenge. How are we to judge whether it is worth the gamble?"

Mr. McIntyre pursed his lips. "I am limited in what I can say, sir. You know that the Cahill family is very large . . . very old. It has many branches. Some of you, until today, did not even realize you were Cahills. But as Madame Grace said in her video address, this family has been instrumental in shaping human civilization. Some of the most important figures in history have in fact been Cahills."

Excited muttering filled the room.

Amy's mind was racing. She'd always known the Cahills were important. A lot of them were rich. They lived all over the world. But shaping human civilization? She wasn't sure what Mr. McIntyre meant.

"Historical figures?" Mr. Holt bellowed. "Like who?"

Mr. McIntyre cleared his throat. "Sir, you would be hard-pressed to name a major historical figure in the last few centuries who was *not* a member of this family."

"Abraham Lincoln," Cousin Ingrid shouted out. "Eleanor Roosevelt."

"Yes," Mr. McIntyre said simply. "And yes."

A stunned silence fell in the room.

"Harry Houdini!" Madison Holt shouted.

"Lewis and Clark!" her sister, Reagan, suggested.

"Yes, yes, and yes," Mr. McIntyre said.

"Oh, come on!" Mr. Holt yelled. "That's impossible!"

"I agree!" Uncle José said. "You're putting us on, McIntyre."

"I am completely serious," the old lawyer assured him. "And yet, all the previous accomplishments of the Cahill clan are nothing compared to the challenge that now faces you. It is the time for you to discover the greatest secret of the Cahills, to become the most powerful members of the family in history — or to die trying."

Amy felt something cold and heavy in her stomach, like she'd swallowed a cannonball. How could she be related to all those famous people? How could Grace possibly have thought Amy could become more powerful than them? She got nervous just thinking about it. There was no way she'd have the courage for a dangerous quest.

But if she and Dan didn't accept the challenge . . . She remembered Beatrice clutching their arms, telling them to take the money. Beatrice would find a way to steal their two million dollars. Amy wouldn't be able to stand up to her. They would go back to their dreary little apartment and nothing would change, except Grace would be gone. No weekend trips to look forward to, nothing to remember her by. Amy never thought anything could be worse than when her parents died, but *this* was. She and Dan were totally alone. The only way out was this crazy idea that they were part of a great historical family . . . part of some mysterious contest. Amy's hands started to sweat.

"Embarking on this quest," Mr. McIntyre was saying, "will lead you to the treasure. But *only* one of you will attain it. One individual"—his eyes flickered across Amy's face—"or one team will find the treasure. I can tell you no more. I do not, myself, know where the chase will lead. I can only start you on the path, monitor your progress, and provide some small measure of guidance. Now—who will choose first?"

Aunt Beatrice stood. "This is ridiculous. Any of you who play this silly game are fools. I'll take the money!"

Mr. McIntyre nodded. "As you wish, madam. As soon as you leave this room, the numbers on your voucher will become active. You may withdraw your money from the Royal Bank of Scotland at your leisure. Who's next?"

Several more stood up and took the money. Uncle José. Cousin Ingrid. A dozen other people Amy didn't recognize. Each took the green voucher and became an instant millionaire.

Then Ian and Natalie Kabra rose.

"We accept the challenge," Ian announced. "We will work as a team of two. Give us the clue."

"Very well," Mr. McIntyre said. "Your vouchers, please."

Ian and Natalie approached the table. Mr. McIntyre took out a silver cigarette lighter and burned the million-dollar papers. In return, he handed Ian and Natalie a manila envelope sealed with red wax. "Your first clue. You may not read it until instructed to do so. You, Ian and Natalie Kabra, will be Team One."

"Hey!" Mr. Holt objected. "Our whole family's taking the challenge! *We* want to be Team One!"

"We're number one!" the Holt kids started chanting, and their pit bull, Arnold, leaped into the air and barked along with them.

Mr. McIntyre raised his hand for silence. "Very well, Mr. Holt. Your family's vouchers, please. You shall be Team . . . uh, you shall also be a team."

They made the trade—five million-dollar vouchers for one envelope with a clue, and the Holts didn't even bat an eye. As they marched back to their seats, Reagan bumped Amy in the shoulder. "No pain, no gain, wimp!"

Next, Alistair Oh struggled to his feet. "Oh, very well. I can't resist a good riddle. I suppose you may call me Team Three."

Then the Starling triplets rushed forward. They put their vouchers on the table and three million more dollars went up in flames.

"Da," Irina Spasky said. "I, also, shall play this game. I work alone."

"Hey, yo, wait up." Jonah Wizard sauntered forward like he was pretending to be a street punk, the way he did on *Who Wants to Be a Gangsta?* Which was kind of ridiculous since he was worth about a billion dollars and lived in Beverly Hills. "I'm all over this." He slapped his voucher on the table. "Hand me the clue, homes."

"We'd like to film the contest," his dad piped up.

"No," Mr. McIntyre said.

"'Cause it would make great TV," the dad said. "I could talk to the studios about a percentage split—"

"No," Mr. McIntyre insisted. "This is not for entertainment, sir. This is a matter of life and death."

Mr. McIntyre looked around the room and focused on Amy.

"Who else?" he called. "Now is the time to choose."

Amy realized she and Dan were the last ones undecided. Most of the forty guests had taken the money. Six teams had taken the challenge—all of them older or richer or seemingly more likely to succeed than Amy and Dan. Aunt Beatrice glared at them, warning them that they were about to get disowned. Ian was smiling smugly. *Perhaps you weren't as important to the old woman as you thought, eh?* Amy remembered what his annoying sister, Natalie, had said: *Grace just knew they weren't up to the challenge.*

Amy's face felt hot with shame. Maybe the Kabras were right. When the Holts turned her brother upside down, she hadn't fought back. When the Kabras insulted her, she'd just stood there tongue-tied. How could she handle a dangerous quest?

But then she heard another voice in her head: *You will make me proud, Amy.*

And suddenly she knew: *This* was what Grace had been talking about. This was the adventure Amy was supposed to take. If she didn't, she might as well crawl under a rock and hide for the rest of her life.

She looked at her brother. Despite how annoying he was, they had always been able to communicate just by looking at each other. It wasn't telepathy or anything, but she could tell what her brother was thinking.

It's a lot of money, Dan told her. *A lot of awesome baseball cards.*

Mom and Dad would want us to try, Amy replied with her eyes. *This is what Grace wanted us to do.*

Yeah, but a Babe Ruth and a Mickey Mantle . . .

Ian and Natalie will hate it, Amy coaxed. *And Aunt Beatrice will probably blow a gasket.*

A smile crept across his face. *I guess Babe Ruth can wait.*

Amy took his voucher. They walked to the desk together and she picked up Mr. McIntyre's lighter.

"We're in," she told him, and she sent two million dollars up in smoke.

CHAPTER 4

Dan felt a dizzy rush, like the time he ate twenty packs of Skittles. He couldn't believe how much money they'd just thrown away.

Ever since he was little, he'd dreamed about doing something that would make his parents proud. He knew they were dead, of course. He barely remembered them. Still . . . he thought if he could just accomplish something amazing — even cooler than making the ultimate baseball card collection or becoming a ninja lord — his parents would somehow know. And they'd be proud. This competition to become the greatest Cahill sounded like the perfect chance.

Plus he liked treasure. And it was a real bonus that Aunt Beatrice's face turned completely purple as she stormed out of the room, slamming the door behind her.

Now the Great Hall was empty except for the seven teams and Mr. McIntyre.

After a tense silence, the old lawyer said, "You may open your envelopes."

RIP, RIP, RIP.

The clue was written in black calligraphy on crème paper. It read:

RESOLUTION:
The fine print to guess,
Seek out Richard S_____.

"That's *it*?" Mary-Todd Holt screeched. "That's all we get?"

"Ten words," Eisenhower Holt muttered. "That's—" He started counting on his fingers.

"Roughly $500,000 per word," Alistair Oh supplied, "since your family gave up five million dollars. I got a bargain. Each word only cost me $100,000."

"That's stupid!" Madison Holt said. "We need more clue!"

"Richard S—," Ian mused. "Now who could that be?" He looked at his sister, and they both smiled like they were sharing a private joke. Dan wanted to kick them.

"Wait a minute." Jonah Wizard's dad scowled. "Did everyone get the same clue? Because my son insists on exclusive material. It's in his standard contract."

"The thirty-nine clues," Mr. McIntyre said, "are the major stepping stones to the final goal. They are the same for each team. The first one, which you have received, is the only one that will be so simple."

"Simple?" Alistair Oh raised his eyebrows. "I'd hate to see the difficult ones."

"However," Mr. McIntyre continued, "there are many paths to each clue. Hints and secrets have been buried for you to find—clues to the clues, if you will."

"I'm getting a headache," Sinead Starling said.

"How you proceed is entirely up to you," Mr. McIntyre said. "But remember: You all seek the same end, and only one team will succeed. Speed is of the essence."

Irina Spasky folded her clue, stuck it in her purse, and walked out the door.

Alistair Oh frowned. "It seems Cousin Irina has an idea."

The Starling triplets put their heads together. Then, as if they'd gotten a collective brain flash, they stood up so fast they knocked over their chairs and ran outside.

Jonah Wizard's dad pulled him into the corner. They had a heated discussion and his dad typed some stuff into his BlackBerry.

"Gotta jet," Jonah said. "Later, losers." And off they went.

That made three teams already out the door, and Dan still had no idea what the clue meant.

"Well." Ian Kabra stretched lazily, like he had all the time in the world. "Are you ready, dear sister?"

"To make fools of our American cousins?" Natalie smiled. "Anytime."

Dan tried to trip them as they walked past, but they nimbly stepped over his leg and kept going.

"All right!" Mr. Holt announced. "Team, form up!"

The Holt clan shot to their feet. Their buff little pit bull, Arnold, barked and leaped around them like he was trying to bite their noses.

"Where we going, Dad?" Hamilton asked.

"I don't know. But everybody else is leaving! Follow them!"

They marched double-time out of the Great Hall, which left only Amy, Dan, Alistair Oh, and William McIntyre.

"Dear me," Alistair sighed. With his black suit and silk cravat, he reminded Dan of a butler. A butler with a secret. His eyes seemed to be smiling, even when he wasn't. "I think I'll have a stroll around the grounds and think about this."

Dan was thankful to see him leave. Alistair seemed like the nicest of their competition, but he was still competition.

Dan stared at the clue again, more frustrated than ever. "Resolution. Fine print. Richard S—. I don't get it."

"I can offer you no help with the clue." Mr. McIntyre managed a faint smile. "But your grandmother would be pleased you accepted the challenge."

Amy shook her head. "We don't stand a chance, do we? The Kabras and the Starlings are rich. Jonah

Wizard's famous. The Holts are like steroid monsters. Alistair and Irina seem so—I don't know—*worldly.* And Dan and I—"

"Have other talents," Mr. McIntyre finished. "As I'm sure you'll find out."

Dan reread the clue. He thought about baseball cards, and letters, and autographs.

"We're supposed to find this guy Richard," he decided. "But why is his last name just S—?"

Amy's eyes widened. "Wait a minute. I remember reading that back in the 1700s, people used to do that. They would use only one letter if they wanted to disguise their names."

"Huh," Dan said. "So, like, I could say A— has a face like a baboon butt, and you wouldn't know who I'm talking about?"

Amy boxed him on the ear.

"Ow!"

"Children," Mr. McIntyre interrupted. "You will have enough enemies without fighting each other. Besides"—he checked his gold pocket watch—"we don't have much time, and there *is* something I must tell you, something your grandmother wanted you to know."

"An inside tip?" Dan asked hopefully.

"A warning, young master Dan. You see, all Cahills—if they know themselves to be Cahills—belong to one of four major branches."

Amy stood up straight. "I remember this! Grace told me once."

Dan frowned. "When did she tell you that?"

"In the library one afternoon. We were talking."

"She didn't tell me!"

"Maybe you weren't listening! There are four branches. The Ekaterina, the Janus, the . . . uh, Tomas, and the Lucian."

"Which are we?" Dan asked.

"I don't know." Amy looked at Mr. McIntyre for help. "She just mentioned the names. She wouldn't tell me what we are."

"I'm afraid I can't help you there," Mr. McIntyre said, but Dan could tell from his tone that he was keeping something back. "However, children, there *is* another . . . ah, interested party you should know about. Not one of the four Cahill branches, but a group that may make your quest more difficult."

"Ninjas?" Dan asked excitedly.

"Nothing quite that safe," Mr. McIntyre said. "I can tell you very little about them. I confess I know only the name and a few unsettling stories. But you must beware of them. This was your grandmother's last warning, which she made me promise to tell you if you accepted the challenge: *Beware the Madrigals.*"

A chill went down Dan's back. He wasn't sure why. The name Madrigals just sounded evil. "But, Mr. McIntyre, who—"

"My boy," the old man said, "I can tell you no more. I've stretched the rules of the competition saying as much as I have. Just promise me you will trust *no one*. Please. For your own safety."

"But we don't even know where to start!" Amy protested. "Everyone else just rushed off like they knew what to do. We need answers!"

Mr. McIntyre stood. He closed his leather folder. "I must get back to my office. But, my dear, perhaps your way of finding out is not the same as the other teams'. What do you normally do when you need answers?"

"I read a book." Amy gasped. "The library! Grace's library!"

She raced out of the Great Hall. Usually, Dan did not run with excitement when his sister suggested visiting a library. This time, he did.

The library was next to Grace's bedroom—a big sunken parlor lined with bookshelves. Dan thought it was creepy being back here with just Amy, especially since Grace had died next door in her big four-poster bed. He expected the rooms to be all draped in black, with sheets over the furniture like you saw in movies, but the library was bright and airy and cheerful, just like it had always been.

That didn't seem right to Dan. With Grace gone, the mansion should be dark and dreary—kind of the way he felt. He stared at the leather chair by the window and remembered one time he'd been sitting there, playing with a cool stone dagger he'd busted out of a locked display case. Grace had come up so quietly he didn't notice her until she was standing right over him. Instead of getting mad, she'd knelt next to him. *That dagger is from Tenochtitlán,* she'd said. *Aztec warriors used to carry these for ritual sacrifice. They would cut off the parts of their enemies that they believed held their fighting spirit.* She'd showed him how sharp the blade was, and then she left him alone. She hadn't told him to be careful. She hadn't gotten angry because he'd busted into her cabinet. She'd acted like his curiosity was totally normal—even admirable.

No adult had ever understood Dan that well. Thinking about it now, Dan felt like somebody had cut away part of *his* spirit.

Amy started searching the library books. Dan tried to help, but he had no idea what he was looking for and quickly became bored. He spun the old globe with brown seas and weird-colored continents, wondering if it would make a good bowling ball. Then he noticed something he'd never seen before under the Pacific Ocean—a signature.

Grace Cahill, 1964.

"Why did Grace autograph the world?" he asked.

Amy glanced over. "She was a cartographer. A mapmaker and an explorer. She made that globe herself."

"How did you know that?"

Amy rolled her eyes. "Because I *listened* to her stories."

"Huh." That idea had never occurred to Dan. "So where'd she explore?"

A man's voice said, "Everywhere."

Alistair Oh was leaning on his cane in the doorway, smiling at them. "Your grandmother explored every continent, Dan. By the time she was twenty-five, she could speak six languages fluently, handle a spear or boomerang or rifle with equal skill, and navigate almost every major city in the world. She knew my hometown of Seoul better than I did. Then, for reasons unknown, she came back to Massachusetts to settle down. A woman of mystery—that was Grace."

Dan wanted to hear more about Grace's boomerang skills. That sounded sweet! But Amy stepped away from the bookcase. Her face was bright red. "A-Alistair. Uh . . . what do you want?"

"Oh, don't let me stop you. I won't interfere."

"Um, but . . . there's nothing here," Amy mumbled. "I was hoping for . . . I don't know. Something I hadn't seen before, but I've read most of these. There really aren't that many books. And there's nothing about Richard S—."

"My dear children, may I suggest something? We need an alliance."

Dan was immediately suspicious. "Why would you want an alliance with a couple of kids?"

The old man chuckled. "You have intelligence and youth, and a fresh way of looking at things. I, on the other hand, have resources and age. I may not be one of the most famous Cahills, but I did change the world in my own small way. You know my fortune comes from inventions, eh? Did you know I invented the microwavable burrito?"

"Wow," Dan said. "Earth-shattering."

"There's no need to thank me. The point is I have resources at my disposal. And you can't travel around the world on your own, you know. You'll need an adult chaperone."

Around the world?

Dan hadn't thought about that. He hadn't even been allowed to go on the fourth grade field trip to New York last spring because he'd put Mentos in his Spanish teacher's Diet Coke. The idea that this clue hunt might take them anywhere in the world made him feel a little lightheaded.

"But—but we can't help each other," Amy said. "Each team is separate."

Alistair spread his hands. "We can't both *win*. But this challenge may take weeks, perhaps months. Until the end, surely we can collaborate? We are family, after all."

"So give us some help," Dan decided. "There's nothing here about Richard S—. Where do we look?"

Alistair tapped his cane on the floor. "Grace was a secretive woman. But she loved books. She loved them very much. And you're right, Amy. It does seem strange there are so few of them here."

"You think she had more books?" Amy cupped her hand over her mouth. "A . . . a secret library?"

Alistair shrugged. "It's a large house. We could split up and search."

But then Dan noticed something—one of those random little details that often caught his eye. On the wall, at the very top of the bookshelf, was a plaster crest just like above the front door of the mansion, a fancy C surrounded by four smaller coats of arms—a dragon, a bear, a wolf, and a pair of snakes wrapped around a sword. He must've seen this before a million times, but he'd never noticed that the smaller crests each had a letter carved in the middle—E, T, J, L.

"Get me a ladder," he said.

"What?" Alistair asked.

"Never mind," Dan decided. He began to climb the shelf, knocking down books and knickknacks.

"Dan, get down!" Amy protested. "You're going to fall and break your arm *again*!"

Dan had reached the crest, and he saw what to do. The letters were smudged darker than the rest of the stone, like they'd been touched many times.

"Amy," he called down, "what were those four branches again?"

"Ekaterina," she called. "Tomas, Janus, Lucian."

"Ekaterina," Dan repeated, as he pressed the E. "Tomas, Lucian, Janus."

As he pressed the last letter, the whole shelf swung outward. Dan had to jump away to avoid getting squished into a book sandwich.

Where the bookshelf had been was a dark stairwell, leading down.

"A secret passage," said Uncle Alistair. "Dan, I'm impressed."

"It might be dangerous!" Amy said.

"You're right," Dan agreed. "Ladies first."

CHAPTER 5

Amy could've lived in the secret library. Instead, she almost died there.

She led the way down the steps and gasped when she saw all the books. They went on forever. She used to think the main public library on Copley Square was the best in the world, but this was even better. It seemed more *library-ish*. The shelves were dark wood, and the books were leather-bound and very old, with gilded titles on the spines. They looked like they'd been well-used over the centuries. Oriental carpet covered the floor. Cushy chairs were spaced around the room so you could plop down anywhere and start reading. Maps and oversize folios were spread out on big tables. Against one wall was a line of oak file cabinets and a huge computer with three separate monitors, like something they'd use at NASA. Glass chandeliers hung from the vaulted ceiling and provided plenty of light, even though the room was obviously underground. They'd descended a long way to get here, and there were no windows.

"This place is amazing!" Amy ran into the room.

"Books," Dan said. "Yay." He checked out the computer, but it was frozen on the password screen. He jiggled a few file cabinet drawers, but they were all locked.

Uncle Alistair gingerly picked a red folio from the shelves. "Latin. Caesar's campaign in Gaul, copied on vellum. Looks like it was handwritten by a scribe around, oh, 1500."

"It must be worth a fortune," Amy said.

Dan suddenly looked more interested. "We could sell them? Like, on eBay?"

"Oh, shut up, Dan. These are priceless." She ran her fingers along the spines — Machiavelli, Melville, Milton. "They're alphabetical by author. Find the S section!"

They did, but it was a disappointment. There were ten shelves packed with everything from Shakespeare's First Folio to *Bruce Springsteen's Complete Lyrics,* but nothing with Richard for the first name.

"Something about that . . ." Amy muttered. The name *Richard S —,* coupled with the word *Resolution,* kept nagging at her. They went together, but she didn't know how. It drove her crazy when she couldn't remember things. She read so many books sometimes they got jumbled around in her head.

Then she glanced down the aisle. At the end of the shelf, curled up on a box on a small table, was an old friend.

"Saladin!" she cried.

The cat opened his green eyes and said, *"Mrrp?"* without much surprise, like he was asking, *Oh, it's you? Did you bring me my red snapper?*

Amy and Dan ran to him. Saladin had the most beautiful fur Amy had ever seen—silver with spots, like a miniature snow leopard. Well . . . not so miniature, actually, since he was pretty enormous, with huge paws and a long striped tail.

"Saladin, what are you doing down here?" Amy stroked his back. The cat closed his eyes and purred. Amy knew he was just a cat, but she was so happy to see him she could've cried. It was like part of Grace was still alive.

"Hey, Saladin," Dan said. "What's that you're sitting on, dude?"

"Mrrp," Saladin complained as Dan lifted him up. Underneath was a polished mahogany box with the gold initials GC engraved on the lid.

Amy's heart skipped a beat. "It's Grace's jewelry box!"

Amy opened it up, and there was Grace's personal jewelry, which Amy had loved since she was little. Grace used to let her play with these—a pearl bracelet, a diamond ring, a pair of emerald earrings. Amy hadn't realized until much later that the stuff was real—worth thousands of dollars.

She blinked the tears out of her eyes. Now that she'd found Saladin *and* the jewelry box, she felt like she really was standing in Grace's most secret place. She missed her grandmother so much it hurt. Then she pulled a very familiar piece of jewelry out of the box. . . .

"Dear me," Alistair said. "That's her favorite necklace, isn't it?"

He was right. Amy had never seen her grandmother without this necklace — twelve intricately carved squares of jade with a green dragon medallion in the center. Grace had called it her good-luck charm.

Amy touched the dragon in the center. She wondered why Grace hadn't been buried with this necklace. It didn't seem right.

"Hey!" Dan called. "Look at this!"

Amy found him around the corner, holding Saladin and staring at a giant wall map covered in pushpins. The pins were in five different colors: red, blue, yellow, green, and white. Every major city in the world seemed to have at least one. Some areas were stuck with only red pins, some with green or blue, some with several colors.

"She's been doing voodoo on the world!" Dan said.

"No, dummy," Amy said. "Those must be markers. They tell where something is."

"Like what?"

Amy shook her head. She found the map creepy. "Maybe something about the Cahills?" She glanced at Alistair.

He frowned. "I don't know, my dear. Most curious."

But he wouldn't meet her eyes, and Amy got the feeling he was hiding something.

"Look at Europe," Dan said. "And the East Coast."

Those areas were heavily pinned in all five colors. Amy could hardly see the cities underneath. If these pins represented the Cahills, then it looked like they'd started somewhere in Europe and spread across the world, heavily colonizing North America.

Then she thought: *Europe. Colonies. North America.* The name Richard S— started nagging at her mind again, trying to scratch its way out. A name from the eighteenth century, someone who had written resolutions . . .

Suddenly, she turned and raced down the row of shelves.

"Hey!" Dan cried, as Saladin wriggled out of his arms. "Amy, where are you going?"

"The Fs!" she yelled.

"What for — *failure*?"

She got to the Fs and found it immediately: a tiny book, so tattered it was falling apart. The cover was decorated with a red-and-white woodblock print of Colonial farmers. The title was faded, but she could still make out: POOR RICHARD'S ALMANACK, For the Year 1739, by Richard Saunders.

"Of course!" Uncle Alistair said. "Very good, my dear. Very good, indeed!"

Despite herself, Amy felt flush with pride.

"Wait a second," Dan said. "If this was written by Richard Saunders, what's it doing under F?"

"Richard Saunders was a pseudonym," Uncle Alistair explained.

Dan knit his eyebrows. "A fake foot?"

Amy wanted to strangle him, but Alistair said patiently, "No, my dear boy. You're thinking of a pseudopod. A pseudonym is a fake name, a nom de plume, a disguise for the author. This book was written by a very famous person."

"Benjamin Franklin," Amy said. "I did a report on him last year."

She opened the book. The text was printed in block letters without much punctuation, so it was hard to read, but there were charts, illustrations, columns of numbers. "This is the most famous thing Franklin ever published. Poor Richard was a character Franklin created. He had lots of pseudonyms like that. When he wrote, he would pretend he was different people."

"So we're related to a guy with multiple personalities," Dan said. "That's great. Aren't almanacs for sports?"

"Not this kind," Amy said. "This has facts for farmers. It's like a yearbook with useful tips and articles. Franklin put all his famous quotations in there, like 'Early to bed, early to rise.'"

"Uh-huh."

"And 'A rolling stone gathers no moss.'"

"Why would farmers care if stones are mossy or not?"

Amy was tempted to whack him with the book. Maybe that would loosen the stones in his head. But she kept her cool. "Dan, the point is he got very famous for this. And he made tons of money."

"Okay . . ." Dan fished out the piece of paper with their first clue. He frowned at it. "So we found Richard S—. How does that help us find our treasure? And what's *RESOLUTION* mean?"

"Franklin used to write resolutions for himself," Amy said, "rules he wanted to follow to improve himself."

"Like New Year's resolutions?"

"Sort of, but he wrote them all year round. Not just on New Year's."

"So was that part of *Poor Richard's Almanack*?"

Amy knit her eyebrows. "No," she said uneasily. "His resolutions were from a different book. His autobiography, I think. Maybe the word *RESOLUTION* in the clue was just to help us think of Benjamin Franklin. I'm not sure. . . ."

She turned a page in *Poor Richard's Almanack*. Notes were scribbled in the margins in several different handwriting styles. She caught her breath. She recognized one line of elegant script, written in purple ink at the bottom of a page. She'd seen the same handwriting in old letters—treasures that Grace would show her from time to time. The notation simply read *Follow Franklin, first clue. Maze of Bones.*

"Mom wrote in here!" she cried. "She always used purple pen!"

"*What?*" Dan said. "Lemme see!"

"May I?" Alistair asked.

Amy wanted to hold the book forever. She wanted to devour every word her mother had written in it. But reluctantly, she handed it to Alistair. "I want it right back," she insisted.

"No fair!" Dan said.

Alistair put on his glasses and examined a few pages. "Interesting. Several generations have held this book. These notes here are in Grace's hand. And here, my father's handwriting, Gordon Oh. And here—James Cahill, Grace's father. They were brothers, you know, although Gordon's mother, my grandmother, was Korean."

"That's great," Dan said impatiently. "But why was our mom writing about Ben Franklin?"

Alistair arched his eyebrows. "Obviously, Benjamin Franklin was a Cahill. That does not surprise me. He was an inventor like me, after all. I would imagine most of the books in this library were written by members of our family, whether they knew their true bloodline or not."

Amy was stunned. All of these famous authors . . . Cahills? Was it possible, whenever she'd sat in a library, lost in books, she'd actually been reading the words of her relatives? She couldn't believe the Cahills could be so powerful, but Mr. McIntyre had told them their family had shaped human civilization. For the first time, she began to understand what that might mean. She felt like an enormous canyon was opening up at her feet.

How had her mother known about the first clue, years before the contest began? Why had she chosen to write in this book? What did she mean by the Maze of Bones? There were too many questions.

Meanwhile, Dan was bouncing around in his usual annoying way. "I'm related to Benjamin Franklin? You're kidding!"

"Why don't you go fly a kite in a storm and see if you get electrocuted?" Amy suggested.

"Come now, children," Alistair said. "We have much work to do without bickering. We'll have to read through these notes and—"

"Wait." Amy's whole body tensed. An acrid smell filled the air. "Is someone smoking?"

Uncle Alistair and Dan looked around in confusion.

Then Amy saw it. White smoke was thickening across the ceiling, drifting down in a deadly haze.

"Fire!" Dan yelled. "Get to the stairs!"

But Amy froze. She was mortally afraid of fire. It brought back bad memories. Very bad memories.

"Come on!" Dan tugged her hand. "Saladin—we have to find him!"

That jolted Amy into action. She couldn't let anything happen to the cat.

"There's no time!" Uncle Alistair insisted. "We must get out!"

Amy's eyes stung. She could hardly breathe. She searched for Saladin, but he'd disappeared. Finally, Dan dragged her up the stairs and shoved his shoulder against the secret bookshelf door. It wouldn't budge.

"A lever." Dan coughed. "There's got to be a lever."

Dan was usually good at figuring out mechanical stuff, but they groped around for a switch or a lever and found nothing. The smoke was getting thicker. Amy pushed on the wall and yelped. "The surface is getting hotter! The fire's coming from the other side. We *can't* open it!"

"We have to!" Dan insisted, but it was Amy's turn to pull *him* along. She dragged him back down the stairs. The smoke was so bad now they could barely see each other.

"Get as low as you can!" Amy said. She and Dan crawled through the library, desperately looking for another exit. She had no idea where Uncle Alistair had disappeared. The bookshelves were combusting — old dry paper, the perfect kindling.

Amy pulled herself up on a table and found the jewelry box. *Don't take valuables.* She knew that was one of the first rules for getting out of a fire alive. But she scooped up the box and kept going.

The heat was getting worse. The air filled with ash. It was like breathing in a poison fog. Amy couldn't even crawl fast because she was wearing her stupid funeral dress. She heard Dan coughing and wheezing behind her. His asthma — he hadn't had an attack in months, but this smoke might kill him if the heat didn't.

Think, she ordered herself. If she were Grace, she would never make a secret room with only one exit.

Amy sank to the floor, coughing and choking. All she could see was the oriental carpet — a parade of woven silk dragons.

Dragons . . . like the one on Grace's necklace. And they were all flying in the same direction, like they were leading the way. It was a crazy idea, but it was all she had.

"Follow me!" Amy said.

Dan was wheezing too badly to answer. Amy crawled along, looking back now and then to make sure he was still behind her. The dragons led them between two burning bookshelves and dead-ended in front of an air grate about three feet square. Not very big, but maybe big enough. Amy kicked at the grate with her feet. On the third try it rattled off, revealing a stone shaft slanting up.

"Dan!" she yelled. "Go!"

She pushed him through and realized with a start that he was holding Saladin. Somehow, he'd found the cat, and the cat was not happy about it. Saladin clawed and growled, but Dan held him tight. Amy followed, gasping for breath. Her eyes felt like they were being sandblasted. They climbed up the dark shaft, and after what seemed like ages, Dan stopped.

"What are you doing?" Amy demanded. The heat wasn't as bad now, but the smoke was still thickening around them.

"Blocked!" Dan wheezed.

"Push it!"

In total darkness, she crawled up next to him and together they pushed on a flat smooth stone that was blocking their path. It had to open. It *had* to.

And finally, it did — popping up like a lid. Daylight blinded their eyes. They crawled out into fresh air and collapsed on the grass. Saladin got free with an indignant *"MRRRRP!"* and shot off into the trees. They were lying in the cemetery, not fifty feet from Grace's newly filled grave. The slab they'd pushed aside was somebody's tombstone.

"Dan, you okay?" she asked.

Dan's face was streaked with soot. Steam rose from his hair and his clothes were even blacker than they had been before. He was breathing heavily. His arms bled from a hundred cat scratches.

"Think . . ." He wheezed. "Don't want . . . collect tombstones . . . after all."

Smoke poured out of the tunnel like a chimney, but that was nothing compared to what Amy saw when she looked up at the hill. Her throat constricted. "Oh, no."

The family mansion was a roaring inferno. Flames winked in the windows and lapped up the sides of the building. As Amy watched, one stone tower collapsed. The beautiful stained glass windows melted. The family crest above the main entrance — that old stone crest Amy had always loved — crashed down and shattered on the pavement.

"Amy . . ." Dan's voice sounded like it was about to break to pieces. "The house . . . we can't let it . . . we have to . . ."

But he didn't finish. There was nothing they could do. A section of the roof crumpled, belching a fireball into the sky. Despair crushed the air right out of Amy's lungs, like the house was collapsing on top of her. She reached for Dan and hugged him. He didn't even protest. His nose was runny. His lower lip trembled. She wanted to comfort him, to tell him it would be all right, but she didn't believe it herself.

Then she noticed something that jolted her out of her daze. In the driveway lay a collapsed figure, a man in a gray suit. "Mr. McIntyre!" Amy cried.

She was about to run to his aid when her brother gasped, "Get down!"

He wasn't as strong as she was, but he must've been desperate, because he tackled her with so much force she just about ate the lawn. He pointed up the road that led through the hills—the only exit from the property.

About five hundred yards away, half hidden in the trees, a man in a black suit was standing very still. How Dan had spotted him so far away, Amy didn't know. She couldn't make out the man's face, but he was tall and thin, with gray hair, and he was holding binoculars. With a chill, Amy realized he was watching *them*.

Amy said, "Who—" But she was distracted by the chirping sound of a car alarm being deactivated.

Alistair Oh, sooty and smoky, burst out of the mansion's main entrance and hobbled toward his BMW, cradling something against his chest. He looked terrible. His pants were ripped and his face was white with ash. Amy had no idea how he'd managed to get out. She almost called to him, but something held her back. Alistair staggered past William McIntyre with hardly a glance, jumped in his car, and peeled out down the driveway.

Amy looked back toward the woods, but the man with the binoculars had disappeared.

"Stay here," she told Dan.

She ran toward Mr. McIntyre. Dan, of course, didn't obey orders. He followed her, coughing the whole way. By the time they got to Mr. McIntyre, the entire mansion was collapsing. The heat was like a new sun. Amy knew there would be nothing left to salvage — nothing except the jewelry box she was still clutching.

She set down the box and rolled Mr. McIntyre over. He groaned, which at least meant he was alive. Amy wished she had a cell phone of her own, but Aunt Beatrice had never allowed them to have one. She fished around in Mr. McIntyre's pockets, found his phone, and dialed 911.

"He took it," Dan wheezed.

"What?" Amy wasn't really listening. She sank to her knees and watched as the only place she'd ever cared about went up in flames. She pictured Grace telling her stories in the library. She remembered running down the halls, playing tag with Dan when they were little. She thought of the secret nook in the bedroom where she liked to read with Saladin on her lap. All gone. Her whole body shook. Tears welled up in her eyes. For the second time in her life, fire had robbed her.

"Amy." Dan sounded close to tears, but he put a hand on her shoulder. "You've got to listen. He took it. Alistair did."

Amy wanted to tell Dan to shut up and let her mourn in peace, but then she realized what he was talking about. She got unsteadily to her feet and stared into the distance, where the BMW's taillights were disappearing around a hill.

Alistair Oh had tricked them. He'd stolen the *Poor Richard's Almanack* with their mother's notes — their only lead in the quest.

CHAPTER 6

Dan had always wanted to ride in a police car, but not like this.

His chest still hurt from the smoke. He sat in the backseat of the police car with Saladin on his lap and tried not to wheeze, but every breath was like inhaling sand.

"If you'd just brought your inhaler . . ." Amy chided. But he hated his inhaler. It made him feel like Darth Cahill or something. Besides, he hadn't had an attack in forever, and he didn't know they were going to get caught in a stupid fire.

He couldn't believe the family mansion was gone. He'd woken up this morning sure that Amy and he would inherit the place. Now there was nothing left—just a smoking mountain of rubble.

The police detectives hadn't given them many answers. It looked like arson, they said. The fire spread too quickly to be an accident. They said William McIntyre would be okay. Amazingly, no one else had been hurt. Dan had told the police about Alistair Oh leaving the mansion in a big hurry. He figured he might as well try to get the old creep in trouble. But Dan had said nothing about the thirty-nine clues or the secret library or the strange guy with the binoculars.

"Who *was* the man in black?" Amy whispered, like she'd been thinking the same thing. She had Grace's jewelry box on her lap, and she was twisting her hair the way she always did when she was nervous.

"Don't know," Dan said. "Alistair?"

"He couldn't have been in two places at once."

"Mr. Holt?"

"Mr. Holt's not that old, and he's a lot more buff."

"Aunt Beatrice dressed as a man?" Personally, Dan liked this idea, because Beatrice definitely had the "evil" factor going for her. After all, she'd just *left* them at the mansion without a second thought. But Amy rolled her eyes.

"He wasn't anybody we know, Dan. At least, I'm pretty sure. But he *was* *watching* us, like he wanted to see if we got out. I think he set that fire to trap us."

"Mrrp," Saladin said.

"I agree with the cat," Dan said. "After that man in black and Uncle Alistair, I say we make a new RESOLU-TION. Stay away from old guys."

"We'll have to be more careful about everybody." Amy lowered her voice even more. "Dan, our *mother* was involved in the thirty-nine clues. That writing—"

"Yeah, but that's impossible. The contest just started!"

"It was Mom's writing. I'm *sure*. She said, *Follow Franklin, first clue. Maze of Bones.* We have to find out what that means. This is just the kind of mystery Mom would've loved!"

Dan knew he shouldn't have felt annoyed, but he hated that Amy remembered more about their parents than he did. He would never have recognized their mom's handwriting. He had no idea what kind of person she'd been.

"We lost the book," he grumbled. "We kind of failed already, didn't we?"

Amy traced the monogram on top of Grace's jewelry box. "Maybe not. I have an idea, but we're going to need an adult. Alistair was right about that. We'll never be able to travel without one."

"Travel?" Dan said. "Where are we going?"

Amy glanced at the cop. She leaned closer to Dan and whispered, "First, we need to find a chaperone. And *quickly.* Aunt Beatrice is going to call Social Services soon. We need to get home, get our stuff, and get out. If the police find out we've been disowned, they'll take us to a foster home or something. We'll never be able to find the thirty-nine clues."

Dan hadn't thought about this. He didn't know much about foster homes, but he figured he didn't want to live in one. Would a foster home let him take his collection? Probably not.

"So how do we get an adult?" he asked. "Rent one?"

Amy twisted her hair into a noose. "We need some-body who'll let us do what we want without asking too many questions. Somebody old enough to look like we're being chaperoned, but not strict enough that they'll try to stop us. Somebody kind of pliable."

"Does 'pliable' mean we can lie to them?"

"Mrrp," Saladin said, like that sounded good to him as long as he got fresh fish.

The police car turned onto Melrose Street and pulled up in front of their weathered brownstone apartment building.

"This is the address?" the cop asked. She sounded bored and annoyed.

"Yes," Amy said. "I mean, yes, ma'am."

"You sure there's somebody home? Your guardian or whatever?"

"Nellie Gomez," Dan said. "She's our au pa—"

His eyes widened. He looked at Amy, and he could tell she was thinking the same thing. It was so obvious even a Holt could've seen it.

"Nellie!" they said together. They got out of the police car with their cat and the jewelry box and raced up the front steps.

Nellie was just where Dan figured she'd be—sacked out on the sofa with her earbuds in, bobbing her head to whatever weird music she was listening to while she punched text messages into her phone. A stack of cookbooks sat next to her on the couch. The top one read *Exotic Mandarin Cuisine.* Dan let Saladin down to explore the apartment. Then he noticed the empty carton of Ben & Jerry's Cherry Garcia—*his* Cherry Garcia—sitting on the coffee table.

"Hey!" Dan protested. "That was mine!" Of course, Nellie didn't hear him. She kept jamming out and typing on her phone until Amy and Dan stood right over her.

Nellie frowned like she was annoyed she had to actually work. She pulled out one earbud. "Back already? Whoa—what happened? You're all grungy."

"We need to talk," Amy said.

Nellie blinked, which was pretty cool to watch since her eyes were done in blue glitter eye shadow. She had a new nose ring shaped like a silver snake. Dan wondered why she wanted a snake curled inside her nostril.

"What do we need to talk about, kiddo?" she asked.

Amy looked like she wanted to hit Nellie with the jewelry box. Dan knew she hated it when Nellie called her kiddo, but she kept her voice polite.

"We—we've got a deal for you. A new babysitting deal. It pays a lot of money."

Nellie pulled out her other earbud. They had her attention now. Three words always worked with Nellie: guys, food, and money.

She stood up. She was wearing her ripped British flag T-shirt, faded jeans, and pink plastic shoes. Her hair looked like a pile of wet straw—half black, half blond.

She folded her arms and looked down at Amy. "Okay. What kind of deal?"

Dan was afraid Amy would freeze up, but she seemed to be keeping her nerves pretty well. Nellie wasn't as intimidating as some of the other au pairs they'd had.

"Um . . . it's a trip," Amy said. "You'd be our chaperone."

Nellie frowned. "Why isn't your aunt asking me about this?"

"Oh, she broke her neck," Dan blurted out.

Amy gave him a look like *Shut up!*

"Broke her neck?" Nellie asked.

"It's not serious," Dan said. "Just a little break. She's, uh, going to be in the hospital for a while, though. So she figured we'd better take a trip. We talked to our Uncle Alistair. He said we'd need an adult to go with us."

That last part, at least, was true. Dan didn't know where he was going with this, but he plunged ahead. He figured if he could just keep Nellie confused, she couldn't call him a liar.

"It's this thing our family does," he said. "Kind of like a scavenger hunt. We visit a bunch of places and have fun."

"What sort of places?" Nellie asked.

"Oh, all kinds." Dan thought about the map in Grace's secret library—all those pushpins. "That's part of the fun. We don't know all the places at the beginning. We could go all over the world."

Nellie's eyebrows shot up. "You mean, like, for free?"

Amy nodded, as if she were warming up to Dan's methods. "Yeah, it could take months! Traveling to exotic places where there's lots of . . . um, food and guys. But you wouldn't need to be with us the whole time—just for the adult stuff like buying airline tickets and checking into hotels and stuff. You'd have a lot of time on your own."

Yes, please, Dan thought. Nellie was okay, but the last thing he wanted was her following them around too closely.

"How are you going to pay for it?" Nellie said suspiciously.

Amy opened the jewelry box and dumped it on the table. The pearl bracelet, the diamond ring, and the emerald earrings glittered.

Nellie's mouth dropped open. "Oh—my—god. Did you steal that?"

"No!" Amy said. "It's from our grandmother! She wanted us to take this trip. She said so in her will."

Dan felt impressed. That wasn't exactly a lie, either.

Nellie stared at the jewelry. Then she picked up her phone and dialed.

Dan tensed. He had visions of Social Services—whatever that was—swooping in, guys with white coats and nets, maybe, taking them to a foster home.

"Hello?" Nellie said into the phone. "Yeah, Dad, listen, I've got a new job for the Cahills."

Pause.

"Yeah, it's really good money. So I can't make dinner tonight like I promised." Nellie picked up the diamond ring, but Amy snatched it away. "How long? Um . . . we're traveling. So a few weeks. Maybe . . . months?"

She yanked the phone away from her ear. On the other end, her dad was yelling in rapid Spanish.

"Dad!" Nellie said. *"No, claro.* But the fall semester doesn't start for a month, and it's all, like, boring courses anyway. I could just take more hours in the spring and—"

Another burst of angry Spanish.

"Well, if you'd let me go to cooking school instead of stupid regular college—"

Her dad's yelling got slightly louder than a nuclear explosion.

"¿Qué, Papá?" Nellie yelled. *"Lo siento,* you're breaking up. I'll call you when I get a better signal. Love ya!"

She hung up.

"He's fine with it," she announced. "I'm in, kiddos."

On Amy's orders, Dan was only supposed to pack one bag. That meant clothes, but Dan wasn't interested in clothes. He looked around his room, trying to figure out what to take from his collections.

His bedroom was already way too small for his stuff. Against one wall were his tombstone rubbings. He'd have to roll them up or fold them to pack them, and that would ruin them. His closet was stacked with plastic bins holding his card collection and coin portfolios — too many to choose from. Under his bed were boxes full of old Civil War weapons, his casts, his autographed celebrity photos, and a ton of other stuff.

He picked up his laptop, which he'd bought from the computer science teacher at school for $300. He'd *have* to take that, because he used it to find out stuff and make money. He knew the exact value of every trading card on the Internet. He'd learned to sell his duplicate cards at school and in the local card shops for a little more than he'd paid. It wasn't much, but he could make about $100 a month if he was lucky. And he *was* lucky. Unfortunately, he spent the money on rare stuff as fast as he made it.

He slipped the computer into his black duffel bag. Then he added three extra shirts, pants, underwear, a toothbrush, his inhaler, and — finally — his passport.

Their parents had gotten them passports right before they died, when Dan was four. Dan didn't remember why. They'd never used them. Grace had insisted on renewing them last year, which had seemed kind of silly to Dan at the time. Now he wondered. . . .

He shoved the passport to the bottom of the bag. There was hardly any room left.

No way could he fit even a tenth of his stuff.

He dug under his mattress and brought out his photo album. It was a big white binder holding his most important collection: photos of his parents.

There was only one. It was burned around the edges: the only photograph that had survived the fire. His mom and dad were standing on the summit of a mountain with their arms around each other, smiling for the camera. They both wore Gortex parkas and thermal climbing pants, with harnesses around their waists. Instead of helmets, they wore baseball caps, so their eyes were hidden in shadows. His dad, Arthur, was tall and tan with salt-and-pepper hair and a nice smile. Dan wondered if he would look like that when he got older. His mom, Hope, had reddish-brown hair like Amy's. She was a little younger than their dad, and Dan thought she was very pretty. Her hat was an Orioles cap. His dad's was a Red Sox. Dan wondered if that was random, or if those were their favorite teams, and if they ever fought about which one was better. He didn't know. He didn't even know if they had green eyes like he did, because the caps hid their faces.

He wanted to collect other photos of them. He wanted to know where else they traveled and what they wore. He wanted to see a picture that had *him* in it. But there was nothing to collect. Everything from their old house had burned, and Grace always insisted she had no photographs of them, though Dan never understood why.

He stared at the photo and got a sinking feeling in the pit of his stomach. He thought about the fire at Grace's mansion, the man in black, Mr. McIntyre lying on the pavement, Uncle Alistair driving away like a madman, and his mom's handwriting in that Benjamin Franklin book.

What could be so important about a book? Dan knew the value of a lot of collectibles, but he'd never heard of anything worth burning down a house.

Grace must've known what she was doing, setting up this contest. She wouldn't have let him and Amy down. Dan told himself that over and over, trying to believe it.

There was a knock on his door. He took the plastic sleeve with the photograph out of the album and slipped it in his bag. He zipped it shut just as the door opened.

"Hey, dweeb," Amy said, but she didn't really sound mean. "You almost done?"

"Yeah. Yeah, I'm good."

She'd taken a shower and changed clothes — back into her regular jeans and green T-shirt. She frowned at his full duffel bag, then looked at all the bins sitting in the closet. Dan guessed she could tell he hadn't sorted through them.

"You could, uh, take a backpack, too," she offered. "If that helps."

Coming from Amy, it was a pretty nice thing to say. But Dan stared at his closet. Somehow he knew he wouldn't be coming back here ever again. "Amy, how much money do you think we'll get for the jewelry?"

Her hand went to her neck, and Dan realized she was wearing Grace's jade necklace. "Um . . . I don't know."

Dan understood why she looked guilty. He wasn't an expert at jewelry prices, but he figured that necklace was one of the most expensive pieces in the box. If she kept it, they wouldn't get nearly as much.

"They'll rip us off," he warned. "We don't have time to do it right. And anyway, we're just kids. We'll have to take the jewelry to somebody who can give us cash without asking a lot of questions. We'll probably only get a few thousand—a fraction of what the stuff is worth."

"We'll need transportation for three people," Amy said uncertainly. "And hotels. And food."

Dan took a deep breath. "I'm going to sell my cards and coins. There's a shop down on the square—"

"Dan! You've spent years collecting that stuff!"

"It'll double our money. The store will rip me off, but I can get three thousand easy for all of it."

Amy stared at him like he'd dropped in from outer space. "Dan, I think the smoke messed up your brain. Are you *sure*?"

For some weird reason, he was. He wanted to go on this clue hunt more than he wanted his collection. He wanted to get back at whoever had burned down Grace's house. He wanted to find the secret of the thirty-nine clues. Most of all, he wanted to finally use that stupid passport and make his parents proud. Maybe along the way he'd find new photos for his album.

"I'm sure," he said.

Amy did something completely disgusting. She hugged him.

"Gross!" Dan protested.

He pushed her away. Amy was smiling, but she had tears in her eyes.

"Maybe you're not such a dweeb," she said.

"Yeah, well, stop crying already, and let's get out of — wait, where are we going?"

"Tonight a hotel in town," she said. "Then tomorrow . . . I've got an idea about Ben Franklin."

"But you don't have the book anymore."

"I didn't need the book for this. Mom's note said *'Follow Franklin.'* Ben Franklin started as a printer here in Boston, when he was a teenager working for his brother."

"So we just look around town?"

Amy shook her head. "That's what the others are probably doing. But we're going to follow where he went next, like follow his life. Benjamin Franklin didn't stay in Boston. When he was seventeen, he ran away from his brother's shop and started his own printing business in another city."

"So we run away, too! We follow Franklin!"

"Exactly," Amy said. "I just hope nobody else has thought of that yet. We need to book three train tickets to Philadelphia."

"Philadelphia," Dan repeated. The only things he knew about Philadelphia were the Liberty Bell and the Phillies. "So when we get there, what do we look for?"

Amy touched the jade necklace like it might protect her. "I'm guessing a secret that could get us killed."

CHAPTER 7

A mile away in Copley Square, Irina Spasky—code name Team Five—was worrying about her poison. She had loaded her fingernail injectors with the usual mixture, but she feared it would not be enough for this meeting.

Back in the Cold War, she and her KGB colleagues used poison-injecting umbrellas, or spray painted toxins on toilet seats. Those were the good old days! Now Irina worked by herself, so she had to keep things simple. The needles extended when she bent back her fingers at the first joint. They were almost impossible to see and caused only a tiny pinprick sensation. The poison would leave her victims very sick, perhaps paralyzed, for many days—enough to give Irina a good head start in the search. Best of all, the poison was completely untraceable and had no antidote.

Unfortunately, it was slow-acting. Her victims might not show symptoms for eight hours or more. If she needed to incapacitate her enemies quickly, she would have to rely on other means.

Ian and Natalie Kabra were not to be underestimated. Back when they were ten and seven, perhaps Irina could've overpowered them. Now they were fourteen and eleven . . . a very different story indeed.

She wandered Copley Square, waiting to spot them. They had agreed on standard antisurveillance tactics, only setting a general area and time for their rendezvous. The storm clouds had cleared. It was a beautiful summer afternoon, which Irina hated. All this sunshine and flowers and children playing — *bah*. She preferred a steel-gray winter in St. Petersburg, a much better climate for espionage.

She bought a coffee from a street kiosk, then spotted Ian and Natalie across the plaza, walking in front of Trinity Church. Their eyes met hers briefly and they kept walking.

Irina's move. She followed them at a distance, checking to see if they had grown a "tail" — any surveillance, any followers, any possible angles for photographers. After fifteen minutes, she saw nothing. She waited for them to turn and see her.

As soon as they did, Irina turned and walked off. The game reversed. She led them across the plaza, toward the library, knowing they would be watching for tails on her. If they saw anything, Ian and Natalie would disappear. The meeting would be aborted.

After fifteen minutes, Irina changed course and noticed the Kabras across Boylston Street, still shadowing her. This meant she was clean. No surveillance. The children turned toward the Copley Plaza Hotel, and Irina followed.

They met in the busy lobby, where neither party could ambush the other.

Natalie and Ian looked much too relaxed, sitting across from each other on overstuffed sofas. The little brats had changed out of their funeral suits—Ian wore a sky-blue polo shirt, beige trousers, and tasseled loafers; Natalie wore a white linen dress that showed off her coffee skin. Their eyes glittered like amber. They were so lovely they made heads turn, which was not a good thing for a secret meeting.

"You attract too much attention," Irina scolded. "You should be uglier."

Natalie laughed. "Is that what keeps you alive, dear cousin?"

Irina wanted to scratch the young whelp's face with her poison fingernails, but she kept her cool. "Insult me as you will. It gets us nowhere."

"True," Ian said. "We have a mutual problem. Please, sit."

Irina considered. She would have to sit next to either Ian or Natalie, and neither was safe. She chose the young girl. Perhaps she would be easier to overwhelm if it came to that. Natalie smiled and made room for her on the sofa.

"Have you considered our proposal?" Ian asked.

Irina had thought of nothing else since the text message came two hours ago on her cell phone, encrypted in an algorithmic code used only by the Lucians.

She nodded. "You have come to the same conclusion as I. The second clue is not in Boston."

"Exactly," Ian said. "We've told our parents to charter us a private jet. We'll be off within the hour."

Chartering a private jet, Irina thought resentfully. She knew the Kabras' parents from the old days. They were internationally known art collectors. Once they had been dangerous people, important people within the Lucian branch. Now they were retired in London and did nothing but dote upon their children. They let Ian and Natalie do all the traveling, writing them blank checks as needed.

What did these brats care about the thirty-nine clues? This was just another adventure to them. Irina had her own reasons for hunting the treasure — much more personal reasons. The Kabras were too rich, too smart, too proud. Someday, Irina would change that.

"So," Irina said, "where will you go?"

Ian sat forward and laced his hands. He didn't look fourteen years old. When he smiled, he looked evil enough to be an adult. "You know it's about Benjamin Franklin."

"Yes."

"Then you know where we're going, and you know what we're after."

"You also know," Natalie purred, "that we can't allow the secret to fall into anyone else's hands. As Lucians, we should work together. You should set the trap."

Irina's eye twitched, the way it did when she was nervous. She hated that it did this, but she could not stop it. "You could set the trap yourselves," she said.

Natalie shook her head. "They would suspect *us*. You, on the other hand, can lure them to their doom."

Irina hesitated, trying to see a flaw in the plan. "What is in this for me?"

"They're our biggest threat," Ian pointed out. "They may not realize it yet, but they will in time. We have to eliminate them quickly. It'll benefit all of us. Besides, you'll have the Lucian stronghold at your disposal. Afterwards, there will be time to fight each other. Now, we must destroy our competition."

"And the Madrigals?" Irina asked.

She thought she saw a ripple of nervousness cross Ian's face, but it passed quickly. "One enemy at a time, cousin."

Irina hated to admit it, but the boy had a point. She examined her fingernails, casually making sure that each of her poison needles was primed and ready.

"Does it seem odd to you," she asked slowly, "that the Lucian database contains so little about Franklin?" She knew very well they would have logged into the branch's mainframe, just as she had done.

Annoyance flickered in Ian's eyes. "There should have been more, it's true. Apparently, Franklin was hiding something . . . even from his kin."

Natalie smiled coldly at her brother. "A Lucian who doesn't trust his kin—imagine that."

Ian waved her comment aside. "Complaining about it will change nothing. We need to deal with Amy and Dan. Cousin Irina, do we have a deal?"

The hotel doors opened. A heavyset man in a brown suit strode through, heading for the front desk. He seemed out of place, possibly a security guard or an undercover policeman. It might have nothing to do with them, but Irina couldn't be sure. They had sat here too long. Meeting any longer would be dangerous.

"Very well," Irina said. "I shall prepare the trap."

Natalie and Ian rose.

Irina felt relieved and perhaps flattered, too. The Kabras needed her help. She was, after all, much older and wiser. "I am glad we came to an arrangement," she said, feeling generous. "I did not wish to hurt you."

"Oh, we're glad, too," Ian promised. "Natalie, I believe it's safe now."

Irina frowned, not understanding. Then she looked at Natalie—that pretty little girl who seemed so harmless in her white dress—and realized the young she-devil had a tiny silver dart gun cupped in her hand, not two inches from Irina's chest. Irina's heart skipped a beat. She had used such guns herself. The darts could carry poisons far worse than she dared keep in her fingernails.

Natalie smiled prettily, keeping the dart gun aimed and ready. "It was so good to see you, Irina."

"Indeed," Ian said smugly. "I'd shake your hand, cousin, but I'd hate to ruin your special manicure. Do let us know when Amy and Dan are eliminated, won't you?"

CHAPTER 8

Amy knew something was wrong as soon as Nellie came out of the rental car place. She was frowning and holding a thick brown padded envelope.

"What is that?" Amy asked.

"It's for you guys." Nellie held out the package. "Somebody dropped it off at the counter this morning."

"That's impossible!" Amy said. "Nobody knew we'd be here."

But as she said it, a chill went down her back. They'd booked the train tickets and the rental car online last night from their hotel, using Nellie's name. Was it possible somebody had tracked them down so fast?

"What does the envelope say?" Dan asked.

"'For A. & D. Cahill,'" Nellie read. "'From W. McIntyre.'"

"Mr. McIntyre!" Dan grabbed the package.

"Wait!" Amy yelled. "It could be a trap."

Dan rolled his eyes. "C'mon. It's from—"

"It could be from anybody," Amy insisted. "It could blow up or something."

"Okay, whoa," Nellie said. "Why would somebody send a couple of kids a bomb? And who is this McIntyre dude?"

Dan grinned. "I say we let Nellie open it."

"Um, no!" Nellie said.

"You're the au pair! Aren't you supposed to defuse explosives for us and stuff?"

"I'm driving you, kiddo. That's enough!"

Amy sighed and snatched the package. She stepped into the parking lot, turned the flap of the envelope away from Nellie and Dan, and carefully peeled it open.

Nothing happened. Inside was a metal cylinder like a flashlight, except the light was a strip of purple glass running down one side. A note was attached in sloppy handwriting, like the writer had been in a hurry:

Meet me at Independence Hall this evening at eight, but only if you find the information.

— W.M.

(P.S. Thank you for calling the ambulance.)

"Find what information?" Dan asked, reading over her shoulder.

"The next clue, I guess."

"What clue?" Nellie demanded.

"Nothing," Dan and Amy said.

Nellie blew a tuft of black and blond hair out of her eyes. "Whatever. Stay right here. I'll bring the car around."

She left them standing with the bags and Saladin in his new cat carrier. Saladin hadn't been too pleased with the cat carrier — anymore than Nellie had been with the fresh red snapper they'd bought to keep him happy — but Amy hadn't had the heart to leave him behind.

"*Mrrp?*" Saladin asked.

Amy reached down and scratched his head through the bars. "Dan, maybe we shouldn't make that rendez-vous. Mr. McIntyre told us not to trust anyone."

"But the note is from *him*!"

"It could be a trick."

"That makes it even better! We've got to go!"

Amy twisted her hair. She hated it when Dan didn't take her seriously. And this could be *dangerous*. "If we go, it says we have to find information first."

"But you know where to look, right? You're smart and stuff."

Smart and stuff. Like that's all they needed to track down a clue in a huge city. Before they'd left Boston, she'd splurged and bought some books about Franklin and Philadelphia from her friends at the used bookshop. She'd spent the whole train trip reading, but still. . . .

"I've got a few ideas," she admitted. "But I don't know where we're going in the long term. I mean — have you thought about what this ultimate treasure could be?"

"Something cool."

"Oh, that's real helpful. I mean, what could make somebody the most powerful Cahill in history? And why thirty-nine clues?"

Dan shrugged. "Thirty-nine is a sweet number. It's thirteen times three. It's also the sum of five prime numbers in a row—3, 5, 7, 11, 13. *And* if you add the first three powers of three, 3^1 plus 3^2 plus 3^3, you get thirty-nine."

Amy stared at him. "How did you know that?"

"What do you mean? It's obvious."

Amy shook her head in dismay. Dan acted like a doofus most of the time. Then he'd pull something like that—adding prime numbers or powers of three that she'd never thought about. Their dad had been a mathematics professor, and Dan apparently had inherited all of his number sense. Amy had enough trouble remembering phone numbers.

She held up the weird metal cylinder Mr. McIntyre had sent them. She switched it on and the light glowed purple.

"What *is* that thing?" Dan asked.

"I don't know," Amy said. "But I have a feeling we'd better figure it out before eight o'clock."

Amy hated cars almost as much as she hated crowds. She promised herself that when she got older she'd live somewhere where she never had to drive. Part of that was because she'd been in the car with Nellie before.

Nellie had rented a Toyota hybrid. She said it was more environmental, which was fine with Amy, but it cost two hundred and fifty-eight dollars a day, and the way Nellie raced around corners and gunned the gas wasn't exactly "green."

They were on Interstate 95, heading into downtown, when Amy happened to look behind them. She wasn't sure why—a prickling sensation on her neck like she was being watched. In fact, she was.

"We're being followed," she announced.

"What?" Dan said.

"Five cars back," Amy said. "Gray Mercedes. It's the Starlings."

"A Starbucks?" Nellie said excitedly. "Where?"

"Starlings," Amy corrected. "Our relatives. Ned, Ted, and Sinead."

Nellie snorted. "That's not really their names."

"I'm not joking," Amy said. "It's, um, part of the scavenger hunt. Nellie, we can't let them follow us. We have to lose them."

Nellie didn't need to be told twice. She yanked the wheel to the right and the Toyota careened across three lanes of traffic. Saladin yowled. Just as they were about to slam into the safety-impact barrels, Nellie slipped onto an exit ramp.

The last view Amy got of the Starlings was Sinead's freckled face pressed against the window of the

Mercedes, her jaw hanging open as she watched Amy and Dan get away.

"Is that lost enough?" Nellie asked.

"*Mrrp!*" Saladin protested.

"You could've killed us!" Dan had a big grin on his face. "Do that again!"

"No!" Amy said. "Locust Street. And hurry!"

Their first stop was the Library Company of Philadelphia, a big redbrick building in the middle of downtown. Amy and Dan asked Nellie to wait in the car with Saladin. Then they walked up the front steps.

"Oh, boy, another library," Dan said. "We have such great luck with libraries."

"Franklin founded this place," Amy told him. "It's got a lot of books from his personal collection. If we can convince the librarians—"

"What's the big deal with Benjamin Franklin, anyway? I mean, so the guy invented electricity or whatever. That was hundreds of years ago."

"He didn't *invent* electricity," Amy said, trying not to sound too annoyed. "He discovered that lightning was the same stuff as electricity. He invented lightning rods to protect buildings and experimented with batteries and—"

"*I* do that. Have you ever put one on your tongue?"

"You're an idiot. The thing is Franklin was famous for *a lot* of reasons. He started out getting rich with his printing business. Then he became a scientist and invented a bunch of stuff. Later he helped write the Declaration of Independence and the Constitution. He was even an ambassador to England and France. He was brilliant. World famous. Everybody liked him, and he lived until he was, like, in his eighties."

"Superman," Dan said.

"Pretty much."

"So do you think he knew what it was — this treasure we're looking for?"

Amy hadn't thought of that. Franklin had been one of the most influential people in history. If he was a Cahill, and he knew about this secret family treasure . . .

"I think," she said, "we'd better find out."

She pushed open the doors and led Dan inside.

Fortunately, the librarians were having a slow day, and Amy wasn't shy around them at all. She loved librarians. When she told them she was doing a summer research project on Benjamin Franklin and needed to use historical documents, they fell all over themselves to help her.

They made Amy and Dan wear latex gloves and sit in a climate-controlled reading room while they brought out old books to look at.

The librarian set the first one down and Amy gasped. "This is Franklin's first cartoon!"

Dan squinted at it. The picture showed a snake, cut into eight pieces, each one labeled with the name of an American region.

"Not very funny for a cartoon," Dan said.

"It's not supposed to be funny," Amy said. "Back then, cartoons made a point. Like, he's saying if the colonies don't get together, Britain will cut them apart."

"Uh-huh." Dan turned his attention to his computer. They'd been in the library maybe five minutes, and here he was, already looking bored, clacking away on his laptop rather than helping her.

Amy pored over the other artifacts: a newspaper that had been printed on Franklin's own printing press, a copy of *Pilgrim's Progress* that Franklin had owned. So much amazing stuff . . . but what was she looking for? Amy felt pressured, and she didn't do well under pressure.

"Find what you need?" the librarian asked. She had frizzy hair and bifocals and looked sort of like a friendly witch.

"Um, maybe some more, please. Anything that was . . . important to Franklin."

The librarian thought for a moment. "Franklin's letters were important to him. He wrote many, many letters to his friends and family because he lived in Europe so long. I'll bring you some." She adjusted her glasses and left the room.

"Franklin invented those, too," Amy said absently.

Dan frowned. "Librarians?"

"No, bifocals! He cut up two sets of lenses and pasted them half-and-half, so he could see long distance and short distance with the same pair."

"Oh." Dan didn't look impressed. He went back to playing on his laptop. He had the mystery flashlight from Mr. McIntyre in front of him, and he kept switching it on and off.

The librarian brought them a stack of new stuff, including old letters preserved in plastic sheets. Amy read through them but felt more hopeless than ever. Nothing jumped out at her. Nothing screamed "clue."

Suddenly, Dan sat up straight. "I found it!"

"You found what?" She'd assumed Dan was playing games, but when he turned the laptop to face her, there was a picture of a flashlight just like the one Mr. McIntyre had sent them.

"It's a black light reader," Dan announced.

"Oh!" the librarian said. "Very ingenious. We have one of those for our collection."

Amy looked up. "Why? What do they do?"

"They reveal secret writing," the librarian said. "During the Revolutionary War, spies would use invisible ink to send messages on documents that seemed harmless, like love letters or orders for merchants. The receiver would use heat or a special chemical wash to make secret words appear between the lines. Of course we can't damage our documents by spraying chemicals on them, so we use black light to check for secret messages instead."

Amy held up the black light reader. "Can we—"

"I can save you time, my dear," the librarian said. "We check all our colonial documents as a matter of course. There are no secret messages, unfortunately."

Amy's heart sank. They'd wasted their time here, and she still didn't know what she was looking for. She had a mental list of other places to visit, but it was very long. There was no way they could hit them all before eight tonight.

Secret messages. Franklin had written lots of letters to his friends and family while living in Europe. *Follow Franklin.* A crazy idea started to form in her head.

Amy looked at the librarian. "You said his letters were important to him. Is there anyplace else that keeps Franklin's letters on display?"

The librarian smiled. "Funny you should ask. Some of his most famous handwritten documents are show-ing this month at the Franklin Institute down on—"

"The science museum?" Amy shot to her feet. "On 20th Street?"

"Yes." The librarian looked startled. "But how did you—"

"Thanks!" Amy rushed out of the room with Dan right behind her.

It was a quick drive to the Franklin Institute. Nellie wasn't too thrilled to sit in the car with the cat again, but Dan and Amy convinced her they wouldn't be long. They ran inside and found a twenty-foot-tall white marble statue of Benjamin Franklin gazing down at them from a giant chair in the entry chamber.

"Holy almanacs," Dan said. "That's a big Ben."

Amy nodded. "At the end of his life, he was so heavy he had to be hauled around in a sedan chair carried by four big convicts."

"Sweet," Dan said. "I want a sedan chair."

"You weigh ninety pounds."

"RESOLUTION: Start eating more ice cream."

"Just come on!"

The museum was huge. They walked past the memorial and through the ticket area, then followed the map into the Franklin Gallery. It was already late in the afternoon and the place was pretty much deserted.

"Check this out!" Dan picked up a mechanical arm and grabbed Amy's wrist with it.

"Stop that!" she said. "Franklin made that for getting things off high shelves, not annoying your sister."

"I bet if he had a sister—"

"He did have a sister! Dan, we need to find his letters. Stop messing around."

They kept walking. They found a display of Franklin's lightning rods, a bunch of bifocals, and one of his batteries for generating electricity—a wooden crate full of glass jars, all wired together.

"That thing is huge," Dan said. "What is that, like, a double Z battery? And whoa, what is *that*?"

He ran over to another display. Inside was a mahogany box holding a row of closely fitted glass saucers, like a stack of cereal bowls.

"It's an armonica," Amy said, reading the description. "It makes music by rubbing water on the rims of the glasses."

"Awesome. Franklin invented that?"

"Yeah. Says here it was really popular for a while. Lots of famous composers wrote music for . . ."

Amy froze. A tall gray-haired man had just crossed the hallway in the next gallery, heading toward the information desk. And he was wearing a black suit.

"What?" Dan asked.

"Man in black," Amy murmured. "Run!"

She grabbed her brother's hand and they fled deeper into the gallery. They didn't stop until they were two rooms away, hiding behind a large glass sphere that showed the solar system.

"What's he *doing* here?" Amy fretted.

"Duh," Dan said. "The fire didn't work, so he's here to get us! We can't go out the main exit. He'll be waiting to jump us as soon as we try."

Amy looked around nervously for another way out. Then she noticed what was on the wall right next to them. Documents. Cases full of documents — all yellowing parchment, written in spidery handwriting.

"Franklin's letters!" she said. "Quick, the black light reader!"

Dan fumbled in his backpack and brought out the light. They held it up to the first letter and shone it through the glass. The document seemed to be some kind of request for supplies. It started:

Sir,—I wrote to you lately via New York, which I hope may come to hand. I have only time now to desire you to send me the following items, viz.

1 Doz. —Cole's Eng. Dictionaries
3 Doz. —Mathers Young Man's Compan'n
1 Qty. —Iron Solute
2 —Quarter Waggoners for America

Purple light passed over the paper, but nothing happened.

"Next!" Amy said. She was sure the man in black was going to burst in on them any second.

"Whoa!" Dan said.

Amy gripped his arm. "You found it?"

"No, but look! This whole essay— 'To the Royal Academy.' He wrote a whole essay on farts!" Dan grinned with delight. "He's proposing a scientific study of different fart smells. You're right, Amy. This guy was a genius!"

"Dan, you're such a dweeb! Keep searching!"

They scanned four more documents written by Franklin. Nothing showed up. Then, on the fifth one, Dan said, "Here!"

Thankfully, it wasn't another fart essay. The letter was something Franklin had written in Paris in 1785 to someone named Jay. Amy didn't know what it was about. She didn't have time to read it. But glowing yellow in the black light beam were lines between the lines—a secret message in the handwriting of Benjamin Franklin:

> *Soon must I leave*
> *This place of wonder*
> *But I leave behind*
> *What hath driven my clan asunder.*

Below, drawn by hand, was a crest with two snakes coiled around a sword.

Amy gasped. "That's one of the crests from Grace's library—the one with the L. Franklin must've been a Lucian!"

"So this is the second clue?" Dan asked. "Or a clue to the clue?"

A camera clicked. "Either way," a girl's voice said. "Nice job."

Amy turned and found herself surrounded by the Starlings. They wore identical preppy clothes as usual— khakis, button-downs, and loafers. Sinead's auburn hair was tied back in a ponytail. Her brothers, Ted and Ned, stood on either side of her, smiling in an unfriendly way. Sinead was holding her cell phone, which she'd obviously just used to take a photo of *their* clue.

"You lost us pretty well on the highway," Sinead admitted. "Fortunately, there were only so many Franklin sites you could've been heading to. Thanks for the clue."

She snatched the black light reader away from Dan. "Now, listen close. You brats are going to *stay* in the museum for half an hour. Give us a head start or we'll be forced to tie you up. If you leave early, I promise Ted and Ned will find out about it. And they won't be happy."

Her two brothers grinned evilly.

Sinead turned to leave, but Amy blurted out, "W-w-wait!"

Sinead raised an eyebrow.

"Th-there's a man . . ." Amy tried to say more, but the Starlings were all glaring at her. She felt like she'd been submerged in ice water.

"What man?" Sinead asked.

"He's been watching us!" Dan said. "Following us! It isn't safe to go out the main entrance."

Sinead smiled. "You're concerned for our safety? That's very cute, Dan, but the thing is"—Sinead leaned in and poked him in the stomach with every word—"I DON'T BELIEVE YOU."

Sinead and her brothers laughed, then turned and jogged toward the main exit.

Before Amy could even think what to do, a low horrible hum shook the floor. And then: *BOOOM!*

Glass display cases shattered. The whole building shuddered. Amy was thrown against Dan and they crumpled to the floor.

When she sat up, her vision was fuzzy. She wasn't sure how long she stayed there, dazed. She staggered to her feet and tugged on Dan's arm.

"Get up!" she said, but she couldn't hear her own voice.

"What?" he mouthed.

She hauled him to his feet. Together they ran toward the exit. Smoke and dust filled the air. Emergency lights flashed from the fire alarms. A pile of rubble blocked the exit from the Franklin Gallery, as if part of the ceiling had collapsed. On the floor near Amy's feet lay the shattered black light reader and Sinead's cell phone.

And there was no sign of the Starlings at all.

CHAPTER 9

Dan decided that explosions were cool, but not if you were in one.

The whole way to Independence Hall, Amy cradled Saladin's cat carrier like it was her life preserver. Nellie yelled at them for being so reckless. Dan's hearing was so messed up she sounded like she was talking from the bottom of a fish tank.

"I can't believe this!" Nellie said. "A real *bomb*? I thought you were joking!"

Amy wiped her eyes. "The Starlings . . . they just—"

"Maybe they're okay," Dan said, but it sounded lame even to him. They hadn't stuck around for the police to arrive. They'd been so freaked out they'd simply fled, so Dan had no idea what had happened to the triplets. He didn't figure it was a good sign that they'd found Sinead's phone next to a whole section of collapsed roof.

Nellie yanked the wheel and they turned onto Sixth Street. "You guys, this is serious. Somebody tried to kill you. I can't babysit you if—"

"Au pair us," Dan corrected.

"—whatever!"

She pulled the car in front of Independence Hall. The sun was going down, and in the evening light, the place looked exactly like it did in school videos — a two-story brick building with a big white clock tower, surrounded by trees and flower beds. A statue of some Revolutionary dude stood out front. The hall didn't look all that impressive compared to the huge modern buildings around it, but back in the day, Dan guessed it was probably the biggest place in town. He could imagine Franklin and all his friends with powdered wigs and three-cornered hats gathering on the steps to talk about the Declaration of Independence, or the Constitution, or maybe Ben's latest proposal for studying farts. The whole scene made Dan think of American history tests, which were almost as scary as exploding museums.

"Look, guys," Nellie said. "The deal's off. Whatever you've gotten yourselves into — this is way too dangerous for a couple of kids. I'm going to take you back to your aunt."

"No!" Dan said. "Nellie, you can't. She'll—"

He stopped himself, but Nellie's blue-glitter-shaded eyes narrowed. "She'll *what*?"

Dan glanced at Amy, hoping for help, but she was still in shock, just staring out the window.

"Nothing," Dan said. "Nellie, this is important. Please. Just wait for us."

Nellie fumed. "I've got, like, six more songs on my playlist, okay? If you're not back in the car when the last song is over, and ready to *explain* things to me *honestly*, I am *so* calling Beatrice."

"You got it!" Dan promised. He tried to push Amy out of the car, but she must've still been in shock, because she held on to Saladin's cat carrier.

"What are you doing?" Dan asked. "Leave him here."

"No." Amy fumbled to cover the carrier with a blanket. "We need to take him."

Dan didn't know why, but he decided not to argue. They hurried along the sidewalk. They were halfway up the steps of Independence Hall when Dan realized the place was closed for the night. "How do we get in?"

"Children!" a voice called. "Over here!"

William McIntyre was leaning against the building, half hidden behind a rosebush. Amy ran over and gave the old lawyer a hug, which seemed to embarrass him. He had a bandage on his left hand and a cut below his right eye, but other than that he looked pretty good for a guy who'd just gotten out of the hospital.

"I'm glad you're safe," he said. "I heard about the Franklin Institute on the news. I assume you were there?"

"It was horrible," Amy said. She told him everything—from the secret library in Grace's mansion right up to the man in black in the museum and the Starling triplets going *ka-boom*.

Mr. McIntyre frowned. "I called Jefferson University Hospital. The Starlings will survive, but they're in bad shape. They'll be recovering for months, which puts them out of the race permanently, I fear."

"It was the man in black," Dan said. "He set that trap for us."

Mr. McIntyre's eye twitched. He took off his spectacles and polished them with his tie, his nose casting a shadow across the side of his face. "This explosion . . . from your description, I'd say it was a sonic detonator. Very sophisticated, designed to stun and cause only localized damage. Someone knew what they were doing."

"How do you know so much about explosives?" Dan asked.

The old man focused on him, and Dan got the sudden feeling he hadn't always been a lawyer. He'd seen things in his life—dangerous things. "Dan, you must be careful. This explosion was almost the end of the race for you. I had hoped to stay out of the competition. I must not be seen as partial to any one team. But when your grandmother's mansion burned down . . . well, I realized just how much of a predicament I'd put you in."

"That's why you sent us the black light reader?"

Mr. McIntyre nodded. "I'm concerned by how much the other teams are targeting *you*. They seem determined to put you out of commission."

"But they failed!" Dan said. "We got the second clue. Nobody else has it, right?"

"Dan, what you found is merely a *lead* to the second clue. Make no mistake, it is a good lead, and I'm glad the black light reader was useful. But it is by no means the *only* lead. Other teams may find different paths toward the next clue. Or, if they believe you have useful information, they can simply follow you, as the Starlings tried to do, and take the information from you."

Dan felt like kicking the wall. Every time they got a break, something bad happened, or it turned out they weren't nearly as close to the next clue as he'd thought. "So how do we know when we find the actual second clue? Is it going to have a big sign on it — CLUE TWO?"

"You will know," Mr. McIntyre said. "It will be more . . . substantial. An essential piece of the puzzle."

"Great," Dan grumbled. "That clears it up."

"What if Nellie's right?" Amy's voice quavered. "What if this is too dangerous for a couple of kids?"

"Don't say that!" Dan cried.

Amy turned to him. Her eyes reminded him of broken glass. They had that shimmering, kind of fragile look. "Dan, we almost died. The Starlings are in the hospital, and it's only the second day of the contest. How can we keep up like this?"

His throat felt dry. Amy had a point. But could they just walk away? He imagined going to Beatrice and apologizing. He could reclaim his collection, go back to school, have a normal life where people weren't trying to trap him in fires or blow him up every few hours.

Mr. McIntyre must've seen what he was thinking because the old man's face paled. "Children, no. You *mustn't* consider it."

"We—we're just kids," Amy stammered. "You can't expect us—"

"My dear, it's too late!" For a moment, Mr. McIntyre sounded really panicked . . . *terrified* that they'd back out. Dan didn't understand why. Then the old man took a deep breath. He seemed to collect his nerves. "Children, you *can't* go back. Your Aunt Beatrice was furious when you disappeared. She's talking of hiring a detective to find you."

"She doesn't even care about us!" Dan said.

"Be that as it may, until she officially turns you over to Social Services, she will get in legal trouble if anything happens to you. If you return to Boston, you'll be sent to foster homes. The two of you may not even be put together. There's no returning to your old life now."

"Couldn't you help us?" Amy asked. "I mean, you're a lawyer."

"I'm helping too much already. Occasional information is all I can give."

Dan's ears pricked up. "Information like what?"

Mr. McIntyre lowered his voice. "One of your competitors, Jonah Wizard, is preparing for an overseas journey. I fear you will run into him quite soon. He and his father made first class reservations in New York this morning."

"Where are they going?" Dan asked.

"If you think about the information you found, I think you'll know."

"Yes," Amy said. "I *do*. And we're going to get there first."

Dan didn't know what she was talking about, but he was glad to see her looking angry again. It was no fun giving Amy a hard time when she was crying.

Mr. McIntyre breathed a sigh of relief. "So you'll carry on. You won't give up?"

Amy looked at Dan, and they came to a silent agreement.

"We'll keep going for now," Amy said. "But, Mr. McIntyre, why are you *really* helping us? You're not helping any of the other teams, are you?"

The old lawyer hesitated. "In the Franklin Institute, you said you warned the Starlings they were in danger."

"Of course we did," Amy said.

"They wouldn't have done the same for you."

"Maybe, but it seemed like the right thing."

"Interesting . . ." He glanced toward the street. "I can say no more. I must—"

"Please," Amy said. "One more favor." She uncovered Saladin's cat carrier, and suddenly Dan realized why she'd brought it.

"Amy, no!"

"Dan, we have to," she said. "It isn't safe for him."

He was about to argue, but something stopped him. He thought about dragging the poor cat up that air vent in the fire, then making him sit through the train ride stuffed in a cat carrier. What if Saladin had been in the museum explosion with them? If the little dude got hurt, Dan would never forgive himself. "All right," he sighed.

"Is that Madame Grace's cat?" Mr. McIntyre scowled. "How did you—"

"He escaped the fire with us," Amy said. "We were hoping to keep him, but . . . we can't where we're going. It wouldn't be fair to drag him along. Could you keep him for us?"

"Mrrp." Saladin gave Dan a look like *You can't be serious.*

Mr. McIntyre had pretty much the same expression. "I don't know, my dear. I am not, well, an *animal* person. I had a dog once, Oliver, but—"

"Please," Amy said. "He was our grandmother's. I need to know he's safe."

The old lawyer looked like he wanted to run, but he took a deep breath. "Very well. For a little while."

"Thank you!" Amy handed him the carrier. "He only eats fresh fish. Red snapper is his favorite."

Mr. McIntyre blinked. "Red snapper? Ah, well . . . I'll see what I can do."

"Mrrp," Saladin said, which probably meant something like *I can't believe you're leaving me with an old guy who doesn't know I like red snapper.*

"Children, you should go," Mr. McIntyre said. "Your babysitter is getting impatient. Just remember what I said before. Trust no one!"

And with that, William McIntyre retreated down the street, holding Saladin's cat carrier out to one side like it was a box of radioactive material.

As they walked back to the car, Amy said, "We're going to Paris."

Dan was thinking about Saladin, and his ears were still ringing from the museum explosion, so he wasn't sure he'd heard her right. "Did you say Paris . . . like in France?"

Amy brought out Sinead Starling's cell phone. The photo of the Benjamin Franklin letter was still on the screen—the secret message a fuzzy yellow scrawl in purple light.

"When Franklin was really old," Amy said, "he was the American ambassador in Paris. He was working on a peace treaty to end the Revolutionary War. He had a house in a place called Passy, and all the French thought he was like a rock star."

"They treat fat old guys like rock stars in France?"

"I told you, Franklin was world famous. He was into philosophy and he liked parties and all sorts of . . . French stuff. Anyway, the secret message said he was leaving Paris, right? The letter was dated 1785. I'm pretty sure that's the year he came back to America. So he was leaving something behind in Paris."

"Something that broke up his clan," Dan said. "That's what asunder means, right? You think he was talking about the branches of the Cahills?"

"It's possible." Amy twisted her hair. "Dan, what I said earlier . . . I don't really want to give up. I'm just scared."

Dan nodded. He didn't want to admit it, but the man in black and the explosion had kind of freaked him out, too. "It's okay. We have to keep going, right?"

"We don't have a choice," Amy agreed.

Before they reached the curb, the door of the Toyota flew open. Nellie marched over to them, one earbud still dangling from her ear. She held up her cell phone like she was going to throw it at them.

"Guess what?" she said. "I just got a voice mail from Social Services in Boston!"

Amy gasped. "What did you tell them?"

"Nothing *yet.* I'm waiting for your big amazing explanation!"

"Nellie, please," Dan said. "We *need* your help."

"They're looking for you!" Nellie shrieked. "Your aunt doesn't even know where you are, does she? Do you know how much trouble I could get in?"

"Throw away your phone," Dan suggested.

"What?" She sounded like he'd just told her to burn money — which of course Amy had already done that week.

"Pretend you didn't get the message," he pleaded, "just for a few days. Please, Nellie, we need to get to Paris and we've got to have an adult."

"If you think for one minute I would — Did you say Paris?"

Dan saw his chance. He put on a sad face and sighed. "Yeah, we were going to buy you a ticket to Paris, plus your pay, and a free hotel room and gourmet meals and everything. But, oh, well . . ."

"Nellie, it's just for a couple more days," Amy said. "Please! We weren't lying about the scavenger hunt. It's *really* important to our family and we promise we'll be careful! Once we're done in Paris, you can do whatever you think is best. We'll swear that it wasn't your fault. But if we go back to Boston now, they'll take us away to a foster home. We'll fail the scavenger hunt. We might even be in *more* danger!"

"And you won't see Paris," Dan added.

He wasn't sure which argument was most effective, but Nellie slipped her phone into her pocket. She knelt so she was looking them in the eyes.

"One more trip," she said. "But this could get me in huge trouble, guys. I want your promise: Paris, and then we get you *home.* Deal?"

Dan was thinking that they had no home to return to, but he crossed his fingers behind his back and said, "Deal."

"Deal," Amy agreed.

"I'm going to regret this," Nellie muttered. "But I might as well regret it in Paris."

She marched back to the car and got in the driver's side.

Dan looked at his sister. "Um . . . about money. I figure we've got enough for three one-way tickets.

We can get to Paris and have enough left for hotels and food and stuff for maybe a week. But I don't know if we'll have enough to get back. If Nellie finds out—"

"Let's worry about that when we get there," Amy said. And she ran to the car, already taking her passport out of her back pocket.

CHAPTER 10

Alistair Oh was just leaving customs when his enemies ambushed him.

"*Bonjour,* Uncle." Ian Kabra appeared on his right. "Have a good flight?"

Alistair turned to the left but Natalie Kabra cut off his escape.

"I wouldn't try to get away, Uncle Alistair," she said sweetly. "It's amazing how many weapons I can carry through an airport."

She held up a china doll in a blue satin dress. Natalie was too old to be carrying something like that, but no doubt she could charm the security guards into thinking otherwise.

"What is that?" Alistair asked, trying to stay calm. "A gun? A bomb?"

Natalie smiled. "I hope you don't have to find out. It would be quite messy."

"Keep walking, *Uncle.*" Ian put as much sarcasm into the word as possible. "We don't want to arouse suspicion."

They strode through the terminal. Alistair's heart pounded. He could feel the *Poor Richard's Almanack* in his jacket pocket, slapping against his chest with every step.

"So," Alistair said. "When did you get in?"

"Oh, we took our own jet," Ian said. "We use a private airstrip where the security is much more . . . relaxed. We just thought we'd come welcome you!"

"How nice," Alistair said. "But I don't have anything you want."

"That's not what we've heard," Natalie said. "Hand over the book."

Alistair's throat went dry. "How . . . how could you possibly know—"

"News travels fast," Natalie said. "We have informants—"

"Natalie," Ian snapped. "I'll do the talking, thank you very much. You hold the doll."

She scowled, which made her face not nearly as pretty. "I can talk if I want to, Ian! Mother and Father said—"

"Blast what they said! I'm in charge!"

Natalie looked ready to yell back at him, but she swallowed her rage. Alistair didn't like the tight grip she was keeping on her doll. He imagined the thing must have a trigger somewhere, and he didn't want to find out what it did.

"Surely you don't want another war between our branches," Alistair said, trying to sound diplomatic.

"One phone call and I can mobilize help from Tokyo to Rio de Janeiro."

"As can we," Ian said. "And I've read my family history, Alistair. The last time our branches fought, it didn't go very well for your lot, did it?"

Alistair kept walking, thinking hard. A gendarme was standing by a security checkpoint up ahead—about twenty meters. If Alistair could create a distraction . . .

"The 1908 explosion in Siberia," he said to Ian. "Yes, that was impressive. But we have more at stake this time."

"Exactly," Ian agreed. "So hand over the book, old man, before we have to hurt you."

Natalie laughed. "If you could hear yourself, Ian. Honestly."

Her brother frowned. "Excuse me?"

Five meters to the gendarme, Alistair thought. *Stay calm.*

"Oh, nothing," Natalie told her brother airily. "Just that you're a terrible bore. Without me, you couldn't even frighten this pathetic old man."

Ian's expression hardened. "I most certainly could, you useless little—"

Natalie stepped in front of Alistair, intent on confronting her brother, and Alistair saw his chance. He stepped backwards, then sideways, and before the Kabras could regroup, Alistair was standing next to the gendarme, talking as loudly as he could in French.

"Merci, niece and nephew!" he shouted at the Kabras. "But your parents will be worried. Run along now, and tell them I'll be out in a few moments. I have some questions for this officer. I may have forgotten to declare my fresh fruits in customs!"

"Fresh fruits?" the officer said. "Sir, that's very important. Come with me, please!"

Alistair shrugged apologetically to the Kabras. "You must excuse me."

Ian's eyes were so angry they looked like they might catch fire, but he managed a stiff smile. "Of course, Uncle. Don't worry. We will *definitely* catch you later. Come, Natalie." He said her name through clenched teeth. "We have to *talk.*"

"Ow!" She yelped as he gripped her arm, but he herded her down the hallway and out of sight.

Alistair sighed with relief. He followed the gendarme gratefully back to customs, where after twenty minutes of questions and searching bags, Alistair realized—*quelle surprise!*—he did not have any fresh fruit in his luggage after all. He pretended to be a confused old man, and the irritated customs official let him go.

Back in the terminal, Alistair allowed himself a smile. Ian and Natalie Kabra may have been deadly opponents, but they were still children. Alistair would never let himself be outfoxed by youngsters like them—not when his own future and the future of his branch were at stake.

He patted the *Poor Richard's Almanack*, still safe in his jacket pocket. Alistair doubted any other team knew more about the thirty-nine clues than he did. After all, he'd been spying on Grace for years, learning her purpose. There was still a lot he didn't understand— secrets he hoped Grace had given to her grandchildren. But soon he would find out.

He was off to an excellent start. He now understood the true meaning of the first clue: *Richard S—'s RESOLUTION*. He had to chuckle about that. Even Amy and Dan had failed to see what it *really* meant.

He made his way through the terminal, keeping his eyes open for the Kabras, but they seemed to have vanished. He got outside and was dragging his bags toward the taxi stand when a purple van pulled up to the curb.

The side door rolled open. A cheerful male voice said, "Hey, there!"

The last thing Alistair Oh saw was a large fist hurtling toward his face.

CHAPTER 11

After getting through customs at Charles de Gaulle Airport, Amy felt like she'd just lost a fight with a tornado.

She'd endured eight hours on the plane, wedged between Dan and Nellie, who both kept their headphone volume too loud. Dan watched movies. Nellie listened to music and flipped through French cookbooks with full-color pictures of snails and goose livers. Meanwhile, Amy tried to make herself small and read her own books. She'd picked up six new ones in Philadelphia, but she'd only managed to finish one Benjamin Franklin biography and two Paris guidebooks. For her, that was terrible. Every muscle in her body ached. Her hair was a rat's nest. Her clothes smelled like airplane lasagna, which Dan had spilled on her mid-flight. Worst of all, she hadn't gotten any sleep, because the more she read, the more an idea had started to form in her head about Franklin and Paris—and the idea scared her.

In the customs line, she was sure she was going to lose it when the official asked about her parents, but she muttered the lie Dan and she had rehearsed — that their parents were coming over on a later flight. Nellie's presence seemed to reassure the official, especially when Nellie started answering his questions in French. The official nodded, stamped their passports, and let them through.

"Nellie!" Dan said. "You speak *French*?"

"Duh. My mom taught French. She was, like, French."

"I thought your family was from Mexico City."

"That's my dad. I grew up trilingual."

"That's amazing," Amy said. She was really jealous. She wished she knew other languages, but she was hopeless at learning them. She couldn't even remember the colors and numbers from kindergarten Spanish.

"It's no big deal," Nellie assured them. "Once you know two languages, learning three or four or five is easy."

Amy wasn't sure if she was serious, but they kept going through customs. They reclaimed their bags, changed their dollars into euros at a kiosk, and straggled onto the main concourse.

Amy felt completely lost with all the French signs. Morning light slanted through the windows, though it felt like midnight to her. Down the hall, a crowd was gathering. People were flashing cameras and shouting questions at somebody Amy couldn't see.

"Oh, paparazzi!" Nellie said. "Maybe it's, like, Kanye West!"

"Wait!" Amy said, but Nellie wasn't going to be discouraged. They pushed through the crowd with a lot of *excusez-mois*. As they got closer, Amy stopped in her tracks. "Jonah Wizard."

He was wading through the mob, signing autographs, while his dad trailed behind like a bodyguard. Jonah wore baggy jeans, a black leather jacket over a white tank top, and his standard half ton of silver jewelry. He looked fresh and well-rested, like his flight had been a lot better than Amy's.

"Le Wizard!" The reporters peppered him with questions. To Amy's surprise, Jonah answered them in French.

There were so many people Amy wanted to melt into the walls, but Jonah looked relaxed. He gave the crowd a brilliant smile and said something that made them laugh, then scanned the faces and locked eyes with Amy.

"Yo!" he called. "My peeps!"

Amy was mortified. Jonah started pushing his way toward them and the whole crowd turned to figure out who he was talking to.

"Oh, no way," Nellie said. "You *know* Jonah Wizard?"

"We're related to him," Dan grumbled. "Distantly."

Nellie looked like she was going to faint. Suddenly, Jonah was right in front of them, shaking Amy's hand and patting Dan on the back and signing Nellie's T-shirt, and the cameras started taking pictures of *them*.

Don't look at me! Amy wanted to scream. *I'm covered with lasagna!* Her voice didn't work. She tried to back away but her legs were frozen.

"Jonah!" his father said. "We should get going."

"Yeah, sure." Jonah winked at Amy. "Come with, cuz. We got stuff to talk about."

Jonah's dad started to protest, but Jonah put his arm around Amy and steered her through the terminal, with Dan and Nellie and a mob of frantic paparazzi behind them, flashing pictures. Amy was sure she would die from embarrassment any second, but somehow they made it outside. The day was warm and overcast. Storm clouds were gathering on the horizon. A black limousine waited at the curb.

"We—we shouldn't," Amy started to protest. She remembered Mr. McIntyre's warning: *Trust no one.*

"Are you kidding?" Nellie said. "A limo ride with Jonah Wizard? Come on!" She practically dove into the limo. A few minutes later, they were gliding down *l'autoroute de l'est* toward the heart of Paris.

"Man, I love this town," Jonah said.

His limo had facing backseats. Jonah and his dad sat on one side. Amy, Dan, and Nellie sat on the other. Jonah's dad typed notes on his BlackBerry, every once in a while looking up and scowling at Amy, like he couldn't believe she was still there.

Outside, rows of gold stone buildings glided by, their windows overflowing with flower boxes. The cafés were crowded with people, all the chairs facing the street like they were waiting for a parade. The air smelled like coffee and baked bread. The cloudy skies gave everything a weird light — as if the city weren't quite real.

"You know my TV ratings here are even better than in the States?" Jonah said.

"Eighteen points higher," his dad piped in.

"And my new album, *Gangsta Life*, is number three on the French charts."

"Number two," his dad said. "And climbing."

"Oh, wow, I love your album!" Nellie said.

"Thanks," Jonah said. "Now shut up."

Nellie looked like she'd been slapped.

"Hey!" Dan cried. "That's not cool!"

"What?" Jonah said. "She's not a Cahill. I'm not talking to her."

Amy was so shocked she couldn't respond, but Jonah just kept right on bragging.

"Like I was saying, I own this town. My art gallery opened last week on Rue de la Paix. My watercolors are selling for six thousand euros a piece. I've even got a children's book coming out."

His dad whipped out a copy and showed them.

Dan squinted as he read the cover. *"Le . . . Li'l Gangsta Livre Instantané?"*

"That means 'little gangster pop-up book,'" Jonah's dad said proudly.

Jonah spread his hands. "See what I mean? I'm more popular than" — he smiled slyly — "Benjamin Franklin."

Something inside Amy snapped. She'd spent several hours reading about Benjamin Franklin, and she was more convinced than ever that he was the most amazing person who ever lived. To think she might be related to him made her so proud. Now to hear this conceited TV star jerk compare himself . . . she was so angry she forgot to be shy. "B-Benjamin Franklin was way more important than you, Jonah! He was the most famous American to ever visit Paris. When he came here, people wore his picture on necklaces—"

"Like this?" Jonah pulled out a Jonah Wizard commemorative photo necklace.

"And . . . and they wore clothes like his!"

"Uh-huh. The Jonah Wizard fashion line is doing great on the Champs-Élysées."

Amy gritted her teeth. "King Louis XVI even put Franklin's picture on a chamber pot!"

Jonah looked at his dad. "Do we have souvenir chamber pots?"

"No." His dad whipped out his phone. "I'll make the call."

Jonah nodded. "So you see, guys, I *am* the biggest thing since Franklin, which is why *I'm* the natural person to find his secrets."

"If your head was any bigger," Dan muttered, "we could use it as a hot air balloon."

Jonah ignored him. "Look, Amy, you're a smart girl. You know the family's got branches, right? Good Cahills. Bad Cahills. I'm—"

"Jonah!" His father covered his phone with his hand. "I thought we discussed—"

"Dad, chill. All I'm saying: I use *my* talents to create *art.* Whatever this final treasure is? I'll use it to bring more beauty to the world! I'm not like those Lucians, man. They're vicious!"

Amy's mind was racing. "But . . . Benjamin Franklin was a Lucian. We saw the snake crest—"

"Okay, so occasionally a Lucian did something right." Jonah waved his hand dismissively. "But today *I'm* the good guy. You gotta see that, Amy."

Dan snorted. "Because you make gangster pop-up books?"

"Exactly! Look, you think it was easy for me growing up rich and famous in Beverly Hills?" Jonah paused. "Actually, it was easy. The point is I work hard to stay that way. Fame is something you gotta keep building, baby. Am I right, dad?"

"You're right, son!"

"I already got albums and TV and fashion and books . . . so where do I go for up? I'll tell you where. I *need* to win this contest. It's a smart career move! If we work together, I'll cut you in for a percentage."

"Uncle Alistair offered to help us, too," Amy grumbled. "That didn't work out."

Jonah snorted. "Alistair Oh? That old fool probably told you how he invented microwave burritos, huh? Bet he didn't tell you he lost his fortune on bad investments. He's nearly broke, girl. He should've taken the million bucks and walked, but he's got some crazy idea the thirty-nine clues are gonna restore his reputation. Don't listen to him. You join me, we can beat everybody. We can even show those backstabbers, Ian and Natalie. You gotta be careful around here, Amy. Paris is a Lucian stronghold, you know. Has been for centuries."

"Jonah," his dad said, "you should *not* be dealing with these people. They have no star power and they're going to drag down your ratings."

"Chamber pots, Dad. I'll handle this." He gave Amy his most dazzling smile. "Come on, girl. We both know the next clue is about Ben Franklin. We could help each other."

What bothered her wasn't that Jonah was an arrogant jerk. What bothered her was that she was tempted by his offer, anyway. The idea of showing up Natalie and Ian was hard to resist. And she couldn't help feeling flattered that somebody like Jonah Wizard was paying attention to her. Still . . . she remembered the way he'd talked to Nellie, and how nice he'd been to them at the airport, but it had all been an act, like they were just stage props for the cameras.

"Why . . . why do you want a deal with us?" she asked hesitantly. "What makes us so special?"

"Nothing!" Jonah laughed. "Isn't that awesome? You're part of the Cahill clan, but you have no talent at all! Me, if I try to sneak into someplace to check out a clue, I'll have the media following me, people shooting my picture and asking me for interviews.

I can't do anything in secret. You — you're so unimportant, you can go places I can't. Nobody cares about you."

"Thanks a lot," Dan grumbled.

"What'd I say?" Jonah looked baffled. "Hey, if it's money, I got plenty of that. I can even throw in a day on the set of *Who Wants to Be a Gangsta?* You can't do better than that."

"No thanks," Amy and Dan said together.

"Aw, c'mon. Just think about it, will you? Where's your hotel? I'll drop you off."

Amy was about to make something up when she glanced out the window. What she saw made her blood turn to ice. It was impossible. What was *she* doing here? And was she really carrying . . .

"Right here!" she said. "Pull over, please!"

The driver did.

Jonah looked out the window and frowned. They were parked next to a seedy-looking hotel called the Maison des Gardons. The awning was tattered and the doorman looked like a wino.

"Here, huh?" Jonah said. "Man, you guys like to rough it. Me, I'm staying at the Ritz. If you change your mind, you know where to find me."

Amy dragged Nellie and Dan out of the car. The driver tossed out their bags, and the Wizards' limo glided away.

"What a creep!" Nellie said. "He isn't like that on TV!"

Dan looked up at the Maison des Gardons. "Don't tell me we're actually staying here."

"I had to get him to stop the car," Amy said. "Nellie, get us rooms for the night."

"Here?" she protested. "But—"

"It says 'gardens' in the title. How bad can it be?"

"Um, that doesn't say—"

"Just do it, please!" Amy felt weird acting so bossy, but she didn't have time to argue. "We'll meet you back here in . . . I don't know, two hours."

"Why?" Dan said. "Where are we going?"

"I just saw an old friend," Amy said. "Come on!"

She dragged him across the street, hoping they weren't too late. With relief, she spotted her target. "There!" She pointed. "In the red!"

Half a block down, a woman in a red shawl was walking briskly. Something was tucked under her arm—something thin, square, red, and white.

Dan's eyes widened. "Isn't that—"

"Irina Spasky," Amy said. "And she's got our *Poor Richard's Almanack*. Follow that Russian!"

CHAPTER 12

Dan was tempted to stop about twenty times as they trailed Irina Spasky down the Rue de Rivoli. (He wondered if that meant "the Street of Ravioli," but he decided Amy would laugh at him if he asked.) A few times he wanted to check stuff out — like the cool glass pyramid at the Louvre and the street performers who were juggling fire outside the Tuileries garden. There was also a vendor selling crème glacée, and Dan was pretty sure that meant ice cream. Mostly, though, he wanted to stop because his feet hurt.

"Is she ever going to take a break?" he complained.

Amy didn't seem to be getting tired at all. "Does it seem odd to you that we happened to find Irina Spasky out of ten million people in Paris?"

"Maybe the other 9.99 million aren't wearing bright red scarves!"

"She was walking down a major street, like she wanted to be spotted."

"You think it's a trap?" Dan asked. "How could she know we'd find her? And she hasn't looked back once. She doesn't know we're here."

But as he said that, Dan remembered television shows he'd seen about spies—how they could tail somebody without ever being seen, or appear "accidentally" in a victim's line of sight and lure them into a trap. Could Irina have been waiting for them at the airport? Could she have seen them get in the limo with Jonah and somehow gotten ahead of them?

"Look," Amy said, "she's turning!"

Irina crossed the avenue and disappeared down a flight of steps.

"The Métro," Amy said. "She's taking the subway."

They lost time figuring out how to use euro coins in the machines to get tickets, but when they got down the steps Irina was still there—standing on one of the platforms with the tattered almanac tucked under her arm. The train was just arriving. Dan was sure Irina was going to try one of those last-minute switches, so they waited until the train's doors were closing, but Irina stayed on board. Amy and Dan jumped on, too, and the train pulled away from the station.

They changed trains twice in a really short time. Even with Irina in a bright red shawl, it was hard to keep up with her.

"I don't get it," Amy said. "Now she's moving faster, like she's trying to *lose* us."

Dan was daydreaming about crème glacée. The lasagna he'd had on the plane was long gone, and his stomach felt like it was trying to chew through his shirt.

Finally, after the third train, Irina exited onto the platform. Amy gripped Dan's arm and pointed to a sign on the station wall.

"Passy," she said.

"So?"

"This is the neighborhood where Benjamin Franklin lived."

"Well, come on!" Dan said. "Red Riding Hood's getting away."

Passy didn't seem as crowded as Tuileries. The streets were lined with four-story buildings. There were flower shops everywhere, like a Mother's Day explosion—tulips, carnations, roses, everything that could possibly make Dan sneeze. In the distance, the Eiffel Tower rose against the gray clouds, but Dan was more interested in the smell of food. The whole city seemed to be made up of outdoor cafés. He could smell chocolate, fresh-baked bread, melting cheese—but Dan didn't have time to get any of it.

Irina walked like her dress was on fire. They had to jog to keep up. Amy tripped over a bucket of flowers and a Parisian cursed at her.

"Sorry!" Amy called back.

They turned onto a tree-lined street with ancient-looking mansions. Halfway up the block, a purple van was parked crookedly. It was painted with pictures of balloons and clown faces, and the sign read CRÈME GLACÉE. Dan's spirits lifted. Maybe he could just grab a quick triple-scoop of cherry vanilla to go. But as they got closer, he saw that the van was shut. The windshield was covered from the inside with a silver screen. It was a conspiracy, Dan decided. The entire city of Paris was trying to starve him.

At the end of the block, Irina crossed the street and ducked inside a wrought-iron gate. She walked up to a large marble building that looked like an embassy or something. Dan hid behind a gatepost and watched as Irina punched a security code and went inside.

"Look at the gate," Amy said.

In the center was a gold-lettered sign that read:

INSTITUT DE DIPLOMATIE INTERNATIONALE
INSTITUTE FOR INTERNATIONAL DIPLOMACY
国際外交研究所

"The Lucian crest!" Dan said. "But what's an institute for, um, whatever that means?"

"I guess it's like a school for ambassadors," Amy said. "But don't you get it? That's just a cover. You remember what Jonah said? Paris is a Lucian stronghold."

Dan's eyes lit up. "This must be their secret base!"

Amy nodded. "The question is what do we do?"

"We go in," Dan said.

"Right. Without the security code?"

"5910. I watched her punch it in."

Amy stared at him. "How did you — never mind. Let's go. But be careful. They probably have cameras and guard dogs and stuff."

They squeezed inside the gate and ran up the front steps. Dan punched in the code. The door opened easily. No alarms went off. No guard dogs barked.

"Weird," he muttered. But it was too late for second-guessing. They slipped inside the Lucian base.

The entry hall was bigger than their whole apartment. The floor was polished marble and a chandelier hung from the ceiling. A set of black doors stood in front of them. On the left, a spiral staircase led up to a balcony.

"Look." Dan pointed above the doors. A surveillance camera was sweeping the room. It was angled away from them, but it wouldn't be for long.

Then he heard voices from behind the double doors — someone coming in their direction.

"Quick!" He ran for the stairs. Amy looked like she wanted to argue, but there was no time. She followed him up.

Dan's heart pounded. He'd always thought it would be cool to play burglar and sneak into someone's house, but now that he was doing it for real, his hands were sweating. He wondered if the French still threw burglars into rat-infested dungeons. He'd seen something like that once in a musical Grace took them to.

They sneaked along a second-floor hallway.

"I don't get it," Dan whispered. "Irina must be a Lucian. Benjamin Franklin was a Lucian. Does that mean Franklin was one of the bad guys?"

"Maybe it's not that simple," Amy said. "Look."

Painted portraits hung along the walls — Napoleon Bonaparte, Isaac Newton, Winston Churchill, a few others Dan didn't recognize.

"More famous Lucians," Amy guessed. "Not necessarily good or bad. But definitely a lot of powerful people."

"And we just invaded their house," Dan said.

They passed a row of heavy oak doors, all of them closed. One was labeled LOGISTIQUE. Another read CARTOGRAPHIE. The last door on the right read ARSENAL.

"Sweet!"

"Dan, no!" Amy whispered, but she was too late to intercept him. Dan opened the arsenal door and slipped inside.

A little late, he considered that it might not be a good idea to enter a room full of weapons if there was already someone in there. Fortunately, there wasn't. The arsenal was about thirty feet square and full of amazingly cool stuff: crates of cannonballs, racks of knives, swords, canes, shields, and umbrellas. Dan wasn't sure about the umbrellas, but he figured they did something besides just stop the rain.

"We shouldn't be here!" Amy hissed.

"Gee, you think?" Dan picked up a shoebox-size wooden crate full of glass tubes with copper wires twined around the tops. "Hey, it's one of those Franklin batteries, like in the museum."

Amy's eyebrows furrowed. "What's it doing in an arsenal?"

"Don't know, but I'm collecting it!" Despite Amy's protests, Dan stuffed the battery in his backpack. It fit because the pack was pretty much empty. The only other thing he had in there was the picture of his parents, wrapped in its plastic sleeve, which he'd decided to keep with him for good luck.

A Styrofoam egg carton caught his eye. He opened it and found a single silver orb with little blinking red lights. "This is cool, too!" He dropped it into his backpack.

"Dan, no!"

"What? They've got plenty of other stuff, and we need all the help we can get!"

"It could be dangerous."

"I hope so." He was admiring the shurikens and thinking he might take some of those, too, when a door slammed somewhere down the hall.

"Better know what she's doing," a man said in English. "If she's wrong—"

A woman responded in French. Both voices faded down the corridor.

"Come on," Amy insisted. *"Now."*

They poked their heads out to make sure the hall was clear, then sneaked out of the arsenal and deeper into the building. At the end of the hallway was another balcony, this one looking down on a big circular room. What Dan saw below reminded him of a military command center. There were computers along the walls, and in the middle of the room was a conference table that seemed to be one huge flat screen TV. Irina Spasky was alone, leaning over the tabletop. Stacks of papers and folders sat next to her. She was punching commands on the tabletop, making images zoom or shrink. She was looking at a satellite map of the city.

Dan didn't dare speak, but he locked eyes with Amy. *I want one of those,* he told her.

Amy's expression said *Shut up!*

They crouched behind the balcony rail and watched as Irina commanded the map to zoom in on different locations. She checked the *Poor Richard's Almanack* book, then got out a pad of paper and jotted something down. She snatched up the book and the pad and hurried out of the room — back toward the main entrance.

"Amy, come on!" Dan straddled the railing.

"You'll break your legs!"

"Hang from the edge and just drop. I've done it off the roof at school a million times. It's easy."

He did. And it was. A second later, they were both at the conference table, staring at the image still flickering on the screen: a white targeting icon hovering over one particular spot in Paris. The address glowed in red letters: *23 Rue des Jardins.*

Dan pointed to a ribbon of blue surrounding the dot. "That's water. Which means that little blob she was targeting must be an island."

"The Île St-Louis," Amy said. "It's on the Seine River right in the middle of Paris. Can you memorize that address?"

"Already done." Then Dan noticed something else—a photograph sitting on top of Irina Spasky's files. He picked it up and felt sick to his stomach.

"It's him." Dan showed Amy the photo—an older man with gray hair and a black suit, crossing the street. The photo was fuzzy, but it must've been taken in Paris. Dan could tell from the yellow stone buildings and the French signs. "The man in black is here."

Amy paled. "But why—"

A voice came from somewhere down the hall: "—*J'entends des mouvements. Fouillez le bâtiment.*"

Dan didn't need to speak French to know that meant trouble. He and Amy ran the other direction, down another hallway.

"*Arrêtez!*" a man yelled behind them. Immediately, alarms started blaring.

"Oh, great!" Amy said.

"This way!" Dan turned a corner. He didn't dare look behind them. He could hear their pursuers getting closer—boots pounding on the marble floor.

"Bars!" Amy warned.

The building's automatic defenses must have been activated. Right in front of them, a set of metal bars was descending from the ceiling, cutting off the hallway.

"Slide into third!" Dan yelled.

"What?" Amy demanded, glancing back at the security guards. Dan ran forward and hit the ground like it was a waterslide, slipping under the bars. "Come on!"

Amy hesitated. The bars were getting lower — three feet off the ground, two and a half feet. Behind her, two burly guys in black security guard outfits were closing fast, armed with nightsticks.

"Amy, now!"

She dropped and started crawling under the bars. Dan pulled her through just as the bars clanged against the floor. The security guards grabbed at them through the bars, but Dan and Amy were already running.

They found an open door and ducked into a parlor.

"The window!" Dan said.

A metal mesh curtain was closing over the glass. It was already halfway down. There was no time to think. Dan picked up a bust of Napoleon from the coffee table and threw it through the glass. *CRASH!* He could hear the guards in the hallway shouting over the wail of alarms.

Dan kicked the remaining glass shards away. "Go!" he told Amy. She crawled through and he followed, pulling his left foot out just before the metal curtain clamped against the windowsill. They ran through the garden, climbed the iron gates, and raced across the street. They ducked behind the purple ice cream van and slid to the ground, breathing hard. Dan looked back, but there were no signs of pursuit—at least, not yet.

"Let's not do that again," Amy said.

Dan's blood was racing. Now that he was out of danger, he realized how much fun he'd just had. "I want an arsenal! And one of those computer-screen tables. Amy, we need to make our own secret headquarters!"

"Oh, sure," Amy said, still breathing hard. She pulled some change and bills out of her pocket. "I've got about two hundred and fifty-three euros left. You think that'll buy a secret headquarters?"

Dan's heart sank. She didn't have to be so mean about it, but she was right. They were burning through their money fast. He didn't have much more than she did. They'd given most of it to Nellie for travel expenses, but it still wasn't much. If they had to fly somewhere else after Paris . . . He decided not to think about it. One thing at a time.

"Let's get back to the Metro," he said.

"Yes," Amy said. "Back to Nellie. She'll be getting worried."

Dan shook his head. "No time, sis. 23 Rue de Jardins. We have to find out what's on that island, and we have to get there before Irina!"

CHAPTER 13

Meanwhile, inside the ice cream van, the Holts were strangling each other.

Madison was on Hamilton's back, hitting him over the head with a box of Fudgesicles. Their mother, Mary-Todd, was trying to pull them apart. Reagan and Arnold, the pit bull, were playing tug-of-war with a package of Eskimo Pies. Eisenhower, the weary leader of the family, bellowed, "Stop it! Company, FALL IN!"

Hamilton and Madison separated and snapped to attention, dropping the Fudgesicles. Mary-Todd brushed herself off, glared at her children, then fell into line. Reagan held the Eskimo Pies in present arms stance. Arnold rolled over and played dead.

"Right!" Eisenhower growled. "I will not have this family killing each other over frozen dairy products!"

Reagan said, "But, Dad—"

"Silence! I said you'd get ice cream *after* we finish the mission. And we are not finished until I get a *report*!"

Madison saluted. "Dad, permission to report!"

"Go ahead."

"The surveillance microphone worked."

"Excellent. Did the brats take the book?"

Madison shifted uncomfortably. "I don't know, sir. But they're going to 23 Rue des Jardins, Île St-Louis."

"*If* you got the number right this time," Hamilton griped.

Madison's face turned bright red. "That wasn't my fault!"

"We drove the rental car into the Seine!"

"Oh, and you have all the great ideas, Hammy. Like that stupid explosion that hit the wrong team in the museum! Or burning down Grace's mansion!"

"Stop yelling!" Mary-Todd yelled. "Children, we can't keep arguing with each other. It hurts team morale."

"Your mother is right," Eisenhower said. "The fire at the mansion and the museum bomb were both bad ideas. We should've pulverized the Cahill brats in person!"

Arnold barked excitedly and tried to bite Eisenhower's nose.

Reagan knit her eyebrows. She shifted uncomfortably from foot to foot. "But, um, Dad . . ."

"Problem, Reagan?"

"Well, the explosion . . . I mean, it could've killed them, right?"

Madison rolled her eyes. "Oh, here we go again! You're going soft, Reagan!"

Reagan's face turned bright red. "Am not!"

"Are too!"

"Quiet!" Eisenhower bellowed. "Now look, everybody. We're going to have to use some drastic measures to win this contest. I can't have anybody going soft! Understood?"

He glared at Reagan, who stared glumly at the floor. "Yessir."

"We know Dan and Amy were Grace's favorites," Eisenhower continued. "Old McIntyre is probably giving them inside information. Now they've beat us inside the Lucian stronghold while we were trying to do surveillance, which was *also* a bad idea! Are we going to tolerate any more bad ideas?"

"No, sir!" the kids shouted.

"They think we're not clever," Eisenhower said. "They think all we can do is flex our muscles. Well, they're about to find out we can do more than that!" Eisenhower flexed his muscles.

"Teamwork!" Mary-Todd cried. "Right, children?"

"Yessir! Teamwork!"

"Arff!" Arnold said.

"Now," Eisenhower said. "We have to get that book. We've got to assume those brats have it, or they know what's in it. We need to get to the Île St-Louis, *without* driving the ice cream van into the river! Who's with me?"

The kids and Mary-Todd cheered. Then they remembered the ice cream, and the kids went back to strangling each other.

Eisenhower grunted. He decided he'd let them wrestle for a while. Maybe it would build character.

All his life, people had laughed behind Eisenhower's back. They'd laughed when he flunked out of West Point. They'd laughed when he failed the entrance exam for the FBI. They'd even laughed the time he was working as a security guard, when he'd chased a shoplifter and accidentally Tasered himself in the rear end. A simple mistake. Anyone could've made it.

Once he won this contest, he would become the most powerful Cahill of all time. No one would ever laugh at him again.

He pounded his fist into the van's cash register. Those Cahill kids were starting to get on his nerves. They were too much like their parents, Arthur and Hope. Eisenhower had known *them* all too well. He had an old score to settle with the Cahills.

Soon, Amy and Dan Cahill would pay.

CHAPTER 14

Amy was all in favor of rushing to the Île St-Louis, but her stomach had other ideas. They passed a *boulangerie*, which must've meant bakery judging by the yummy smells, and Dan and she exchanged looks.

"Just one stop," they said together.

A few minutes later they were sitting on the quay of the river, sharing the best meal they'd ever had. It was only a loaf of bread, but Amy had never tasted anything so good.

"See that?" Amy pointed to the top of a nearby church, where a black iron spike rose from the bell tower. "Lightning rod."

"Umm," Dan said with his mouth full.

"The French were the first ones to test Franklin's theories about lightning rods. A lot of the old buildings still have original Franklin models."

"Mmm!" Dan said enthusiastically, but Amy wasn't sure whether he liked the story or the bread.

The sun was going down behind a bulkhead of black clouds. Thunder rumbled in the distance, but the

Parisians didn't seem too concerned. Joggers and skaters crowded the riverside. A sightseeing boat loaded with tourists hummed along on the Seine.

Amy tried to use the Starlings' cell phone to call Nellie, but the phone was dead. Apparently, it wasn't set up to get a signal in France.

Her nerves were still buzzing from their raid on the Lucian stronghold. Despite all the security, it still seemed like they'd gotten in and out pretty easily, and she wasn't sure why. She also didn't like the stuff Dan had taken — the Franklin battery and that weird metal sphere. She knew better than to argue with him about it, though. Once he got his hands on something, he hardly ever let it go.

She wondered how Irina Spasky had gotten the book from Uncle Alistair, and why she would be interested in the Île St-Louis. It felt like a trap, but it was Amy's only lead — or at least, the only lead she wanted to think about. Her mother's note in the *Poor Richard's Almanack* — the Maze of Bones — still gave her chills.

She tried to imagine what her mother or Grace would do in her place. They would be braver. They'd see what to do more clearly. Her mother had once searched for these same clues. Amy was sure of that now. Grace had intended Amy to take up the challenge, but what if Amy wasn't up to it?

So far she felt like she'd done a terrible job. Every time she'd needed to speak up, she failed. The other teams probably thought she was a mumbling loser.

If it wasn't for Dan, she would've been lost. Just thinking about it made a lump form in her throat.

They finished the bread. Amy knew they needed to get moving. She stared at the darkening sky and tried to remember details from her Paris guidebooks. "There aren't any Métro lines to Île St-Louis," she said. "We'll have to walk."

"Let's do it!" Dan hopped to his feet.

Amy couldn't believe how quickly his spirits had rebounded. A few minutes ago, he'd been complaining about his feet and his heavy backpack. Now, a hunk of bread later, he was as good as new. Amy wished she was like that. She felt like lying down and sleeping for a century, but she wasn't going to tell that to Dan.

It was full dark by the time they got to the Pont Louis-Philippe. The old stone bridge was lined with streetlamps that glowed against the water. On the opposite side rose a cluster of trees and mansions — the Île St-Louis. To the north was a larger island, with a huge cathedral lit up yellow in the night.

"That's the Île de la Cité over there," Amy said as they walked across, mostly to keep herself calm. "And that's Notre Dame Cathedral."

"Cool," Dan said. "You think we can see the hunchback?"

"Um . . . maybe later." Amy decided not to tell him that the hunchback of Notre Dame was just a character in a book. "Anyway, the smaller island we're going to — the Île St-Louis — the tour books hardly said anything about it. Mostly old houses and shops and stuff. I don't know why Irina would be looking there."

"No Ben Franklin history?"

Amy shook her head. "It used to be called the Island of the Cows, because that's all that lived there. Then they turned it into a neighborhood."

"Cows," Dan said. "Exciting."

After the other parts of Paris they'd seen, the Île St-Louis felt like a ghost town. The narrow streets were lined with elegant old apartments—five stories tall with black gabled roofs. Most of the windows were dark. A lot of the shops were closed. Streetlamps cast weird shadows through the branches of the trees, making monster shapes on the walls. Amy was too old to believe in monsters, but the shadows still made her uneasy.

An elderly couple crossed the street in front of them. Amy wondered if it was her imagination, or if the couple really glanced at her suspiciously before they disappeared into an alleyway. On the next block, a guy in a beret was walking a Labrador retriever. He smiled as he passed Amy and Dan, but his expression reminded Amy of Ian Kabra—like he knew a secret.

You're just getting paranoid, she told herself. Or was it possible there were other people seeking the clues, people that weren't even part of the seven teams? She glanced at Dan but decided not to say anything about this . . . not yet. The contest was already overwhelming enough.

After another hundred yards, they found the Rue des Jardins. It was narrower than the streets around it, with crumbling stone buildings that might've stood there for centuries.

Amy counted the street numbers. She stopped abruptly. "Dan . . . *23* Rue des Jardins. Are you sure?"

"Yeah. Why?"

Amy pointed. There was no building at 23 Rue des Jardins. Instead, ringed with a rusty iron fence, was a tiny cemetery. At the back stood a marble mausoleum. In front, a dozen weathered headstones slanted every direction like crooked teeth.

The cemetery was sandwiched by tall buildings on either side. The one on the right said MUSÉE. The one on the left must've been some kind of shop once, but the windows were painted black and the door boarded up. The only light came from the dim orange glow of the city sky, which made the place seem even creepier.

"I don't like this," Amy said. "There can't be any connection to Franklin here."

"How do you know?" Dan asked. "We haven't even searched. And those tombstones look cool!"

"No, Dan. You *cannot* do charcoal rubbings."

"Aw . . ." He walked through the cemetery gates, and Amy had no choice but to follow.

The tombstones told them nothing. Once upon a time, they might've had inscriptions, but they'd been worn smooth over the centuries. Amy's pulse was racing. Something wasn't right. She racked her brain, trying to figure out why this place might be important to Ben Franklin, but she couldn't come up with anything.

Cautiously, she approached the mausoleum. She'd always hated aboveground burial places. They made her think of dollhouses for dead people.

The iron doors stood open. Amy was hesitant to get close. From ten feet away, she couldn't see anything special inside — just old nameplates lining the walls — but a slab of marble lay on the ground in front of the doorway. With a start, Amy realized the inscription was a lot newer than the rest of the cemetery. It looked freshly carved:

SE TROUVENT ICI
AMY ET DAN CAHILL
ILS ONT COLLÉ LEURS NEZ DANS
LES AFFAIRES DES AUTRES

"Whoa," Dan said. "Why are our names—"

"Some kind of message . . ." Amy desperately wished she could read French. If she ever got back to the hotel, she promised herself she would make Nellie give her lessons.

"Inside, right?" Dan said.

"No, it's a trap!"

But he stepped forward and the ground collapsed. The marble slab dropped into nothingness, taking Dan with it.

"Dan!"

She ran to the edge of the hole, but the ground hadn't finished crumbling. Stone and dirt gave way like cloth under her feet and Amy tumbled into darkness.

For a second, she was too dazed to think. She coughed, her lungs filling with dust. She was sitting on something soft and warm. . . .

"Dan!" In a panic, she scrambled off him and shook his arms, but it was too dark to see. "Dan, please, be alive!"

"Ugh," he grunted.

"Are you okay?"

"My sister just sat on me with her bony butt. Of course I'm not okay."

Amy breathed a sigh of relief. If he was being annoying, he must be fine. She got up unsteadily, dirt and stones shifting beneath her feet. Looking up, she could see the mouth of the ragged pit they'd fallen into. They were in some kind of a sinkhole.

"The ground was hollowed out," she muttered. "The earth here is limestone. Lots of caves and tunnels under Paris. I guess we fell into one accidentally."

"Accidentally?" Dan said. "Irina lured us here on purpose!"

Amy knew he was probably right, but she didn't want to think about it . . . or what might happen next. They had to get out. She swept her arms around the edges of their pit, but it was just that—a pit. No side tunnels, no exits except for straight up, and they'd fallen over ten feet. It was a miracle they hadn't broken any bones.

Suddenly, a light blinded her from above. "Well, well," said a man's voice.

"Arf!" a dog yapped.

When Amy's eyes adjusted, she saw five figures in purple warm-up suits smiling down at them, and one very excited pit bull.

"The Holts!" Dan said. "It figures. You helped Irina set us up!"

"Oh, get over it, runt," Madison called down. "We didn't set up anybody."

"Yeah," Reagan said. "You fell in all by yourselves."

She and Madison gave each other high fives and started laughing.

Amy's hands started to tremble. This was just like her nightmares . . . stuck in a pit, a crowd of people laughing at her. But this was *real.*

"So." Eisenhower Holt called down. "Is this what you brats were looking for? Is this the Maze of Bones?"

Her heart fluttered. "What—what do you mean?"

"Oh, come on, missy! We know all about the Maze of Bones. We read the *Almanack.*"

"You have the book? But, Irina—"

"Stole it from us," Eisenhower growled. "After we stole it from the Korean dude. So we staked out her headquarters, but *you* got inside before we could launch an assault. Now you've got the book, and you came here, which means you know something."

"But we don't have the book!" Amy said. "We didn't even get a chance to—"

"Oh, come on," Hamilton said. His greased blond hair gleamed in the night. "It was right there on page fifty-two—*BF: Maze of Bones, coordinates in the box.* It was your mom's handwriting. Dad recognized it."

Amy's whole body was trembling. She hated it, but she couldn't stop. The Holts had read farther in the book than she had. They'd found another message from her mother: *Maze of Bones, coordinates in the box.* She understood the Maze of Bones part, at least she feared that she did . . . but coordinates in a box?

"I—I don't know what it means," she said. "We don't have the book. But if you let us out of here, maybe I could—"

"Yeah, right!" Madison sneered. "Like we'd help you!"

They started laughing again—the entire Holt clan, making fun of her.

"Please, stop," she whispered. "Don't . . ."

"Aw, she's gonna cry." Hamilton grinned. "Man, you two are pathetic. I can't believe you got past the fire and the bomb."

"*What?*" Dan yelled. "*You* burned Grace's mansion? *You* set off that bomb in the museum?"

"To slow you down," Eisenhower admitted. "We should've beaten you up in person. Sorry about that."

Dan threw a rock, but it sailed harmlessly between Reagan's legs. "You morons! Get us OUT of here!"

Reagan frowned, but Madison and Hamilton started yelling back at Dan. Arnold barked. Amy knew this was getting them nowhere. They had to convince the Holts to let them out, but she couldn't make her voice work. She wanted to curl into a ball and hide.

Then the ground shook. There was a rumbling sound like a large engine. The Holts turned toward the street and looked astonished by whatever they saw.

"You—little—tricksters!" Eisenhower glared down at them. "This was an ambush, wasn't it?"

"What are you talking about?" Dan asked.

"A truck is blocking the gates!" Mary-Todd said. "A cement truck."

"Dad, look," Reagan said nervously. "They've got shovels."

Amy's danger sense started tingling. Dan turned toward her, and she could tell he was thinking the same thing.

"They're going to fill the hole," Dan said. "Aren't they?"

She nodded weakly.

"Mr. Holt!" Dan started jumping like Arnold the dog, but he couldn't reach the top of the pit.

"Come on, you've got to get us out! We'll help you!"

Mr. Holt snorted. "You led us into this! Besides, you runts can't fight."

"Dad," Reagan said. "Maybe we should—"

"Shut up, sis," Hamilton growled. "We can handle this!"

"Reagan!" Dan yelled. "Come on! Tell them to let us out."

Reagan just knit her eyebrows and stared at the ground.

Dan looked at Amy desperately. "You gotta do something. Tell them you can figure out the book!"

But the words wouldn't come. Amy felt like she was already being covered in cement. Her brother needed her. She had to say something. But she just stood there, frozen and helpless and hating herself for being so scared.

"HEEEY!" Dan yelled up. "Amy knows what the clue means! She'll tell you if you let us out!"

Mr. Holt scowled. Amy knew he wouldn't go for it. They'd be stuck down here forever, cemented in. Then Mr. Holt stripped off his warm-up jacket and lowered it into the pit. "Grab the sleeve."

Within seconds, Amy and Dan were out of the pit. Sure enough, a cement truck had blocked the gates of the cemetery. Six thugs in coveralls and hard hats were lined up at the fence, hefting shovels like they were ready to fight.

"All right, team," Mr. Holt said with relish. "Let's show 'em how it's done—Holt style!"

The whole family rushed forward. Mr. Holt grabbed the first thug's shovel and swung it, with the guy still attached, into the side of the cement truck. *CLANG!* The girls, Madison and Reagan, plowed into one thug so hard he flew across the street and crashed through the window of a flower shop. Arnold bit the third thug in the leg and held on with jaws of iron. Mary-Todd and Hamilton tackled a fourth thug against the chute on the back of the truck. His head hit a lever and cement started spilling all over the street.

Unfortunately, two thugs remained, and they ran straight for Amy and Dan. Fear closed around Amy's throat. She recognized their faces — they were the security guards from the Lucian stronghold. Before she could even think of a plan, Dan unzipped his backpack and took out his blinking silver sphere.

"Dan, no!" Amy said. "You can't—" But he did.

As much as he loved baseball, Dan was the world's worst pitcher. The sphere sailed right past the two guys who were charging them and exploded under Mr. Holt's feet with a blinding yellow flash. The noise was like the world's largest snare drum being smashed with a sledgehammer. Amy went cross-eyed. When she regained her senses, she saw the entire Holt family and the guys they'd been battling flat on the ground, knocked unconscious — except for the two thugs Dan *meant* to hit. They were only dazed, stumbling around and shaking their heads.

Amy turned to Dan in horror. "What did you *do*?"

Dan looked surprised. "Um, concussive grenade, I think. Like the one in the museum! I knocked them out."

The two thugs who were still on their feet blinked a few times, then refocused on Dan and Amy. They didn't look happy.

"Run!" Dan pulled Amy behind the mausoleum, but there was nowhere to go — just another iron fence, and a few yards behind that, the back of a building — brick walls, thirty feet high.

Desperately, they climbed the fence anyway. Amy's shirt got stuck on the top, but Dan pulled her free. Together they pressed against the back wall. There was no alley. No exit. They were trapped. If only they had a weapon . . . and then Amy realized her brain wasn't paralyzed by fear anymore. The explosion had snapped her back to her senses. She knew what they needed. "Dan, the Franklin battery!"

"What good will *that* do?"

She ripped open his backpack and took out the battery. The two thugs advanced warily — probably wondering whether Dan had any more grenades. Amy uncoiled the battery's copper wires and made sure the ends were stripped. "I hope it has a charge."

"What are you doing?" Dan asked.

"Franklin used to do this for fun," she said. "To startle his friends. Maybe if it's got enough juice . . ."

The men were at the fence. One of them snarled something in French. It sounded like an order to surrender. Amy shook her head.

The men began to climb, and Amy leaped forward. She touched the wires against the fence and the men yelped in surprise. Blue sparks flew off the metal bars. Smoke curled from the men's hands and they fell backwards, stunned. Amy threw down the battery.

"Come on!" she yelled.

In a heartbeat, they were over the fence. They raced out of the graveyard, past the unconscious Holts, the thugs, and the overturned cement truck.

Amy felt a twinge of guilt leaving the Holts behind unconscious, but they had no choice.

They didn't stop running until they were halfway across the Pont Louis-Philippe. Amy doubled over, gasping for breath. At last they were safe. They'd survived the trap.

But when she looked back, she saw something that scared her worse than the graveyard. Standing in the shadows at the foot of the bridge, a hundred yards back the way they'd come, was a tall gray-haired man in a black overcoat.

And Amy was sure he was watching them.

CHAPTER 15

Dan thought Nellie was going to kill them. He'd never seen her face that shade of red before.

"You did *what*?" She paced their tiny hotel room. "Two hours, you said. *Two hours*. And I was standing outside the hotel for, like, *ever*, and you didn't come. You didn't call. I thought you were dead!" She shook her iPod for emphasis and the loose earbuds danced around.

"Our phone didn't work," Amy said sheepishly.

"We got sidetracked," Dan added. "There was this concussive grenade, and a cement truck, and a battery. And a loaf of bread."

Dan was pretty sure that covered all the important details, but Nellie looked like she didn't understand.

"Start from the beginning," she said. "And *no lies*."

Maybe it was just because he was too tired to lie, but Dan told her the whole story—even about the thirty-nine clues—with Amy filling in the stuff he forgot.

"So you almost died," Nellie said in a small voice. "Those jerks were going to pour cement on you."

"Maybe a little cement," Dan said.

"What did the inscription say?" Nellie asked.

Dan didn't know any French, but he'd automatically memorized the words on the marble slab. He repeated them to Nellie.

"'Here lie Amy and Dan Cahill,'" she translated, "'who stuck their noses into the wrong people's business.'"

"It was Irina Spasky's fault!" Dan said. "She tricked us into going there. The whole thing was a setup."

"And we can't even pay you," Amy added miserably. "We don't have enough money for the flight home. I'm . . . I'm really sorry, Nellie."

Nellie stood very still. Her glitter eye shadow was red today, which made her eyes look even angrier. Her arms were crossed over her T-shirt, which showed a picture of a screaming punk rocker. All in all, she looked pretty scary. Then she grabbed Amy and Dan and hugged them fiercely.

She knelt down so she was looking them in the eyes. "I've got some credit left on my MasterCard. We'll be fine."

Dan was confused. "But . . . you're not going to kill us?"

"I'm going to help you, stupid." Nellie shook his shoulders gently. "Nobody messes with my babysitees."

"Au pairees," Dan corrected.

"Whatever! Now get some sleep. Tomorrow we're going to slap some people senseless."

Maison des Gardons did not mean the house of gardens. Apparently, *gardons* meant roaches. Dan found this out because Nellie told him, and because he heard scuttling sounds along the floor all night long. He wished Saladin were there. The cat would've had a great time playing jungle stalker.

In the morning, everybody looked bleary-eyed, but they showered and changed clothes. Nellie came back from the corner café with coffee for herself, hot chocolate for Dan and Amy, and *pain au chocolat* for all of them. Dan figured any country that ate chocolate for breakfast couldn't be all bad.

"So," Dan said, "can I get some more grenades today?"

"No!" Amy said. "Dan, you're lucky it was only concussive. You could've wiped out the whole Holt family."

"And that would've been bad because . . . ?"

"Okay, knock it off," Nellie said. "The important thing is you guys are safe."

Amy picked at her croissant. She looked pale this morning. Her hair was a tangled mess. "Dan . . . I'm sorry about last night. I—I panicked. I almost got us killed."

Dan had pretty much forgotten that part. He'd been annoyed with her at the time, but it was hard to stay mad when Amy looked so miserable and apologized.

Plus she'd done that cool thing with the battery, which had kind of made up for her freaking out.

"Don't worry about it," he said.

"But if it happens again—"

"Hey, if we let Irina lure us into a trap again, we're stupider than the Holts."

Amy didn't look very comforted. "What I don't understand is the man in black. Why was he there last night? And if the Holts started the fire at the mansion and set up the museum explosion—"

"Then what was the man in black doing in both places?" Dan finished. "And why did Irina have a photo of him?"

He waited for Amy to come up with one of her "oh-I-did-a-book-report-on-that-last-year" answers, but she just kept frowning at her breakfast.

"Maybe you guys should concentrate on where we go next," Nellie advised.

Amy took a deep breath. "I think I know where to go. Dan, can I use your laptop?"

He stared at her, because Amy didn't like computers. But finally he brought it over and Amy started searching the Internet.

In no time, she grimaced and turned the screen for them to see. The picture showed a pile of bones in a dark stone room.

"I've suspected for a while," Amy said, "but I was hoping I was wrong because it's risky. *The Maze of Bones.* That's what Mom's note said in *Poor Richard's*

Almanack. We have to explore the Catacombs."

"Is that where they keep the cats?" Dan asked.

It seemed like a perfectly reasonable question to him, but Amy gave him a "you're-such-a-dummy" look.

"The Catacombs are an underground maze," she said. "I told you Paris is riddled with caves and tunnels, right? All the limestone they used to build the city, ever since the Roman days, they dug from underground, and it left a whole network of empty spaces. Some are just pits, like the one we fell in last night."

"And some are networks of tunnels," Nellie said. "Yeah, I remember hearing about this. And they're filled with bones, right?"

"I want a room decorated with bones!" Dan said. "Where'd they come from?"

"Cemeteries," Amy said. "Back in the 1700s, the cemeteries were getting overcrowded, so they decided to dig up tons of old bodies—all their bones—and move them into the Catacombs. The thing is . . . look at the dates. See when they started moving bones into the Catacombs?"

Dan squinted at the screen. He didn't see what she was talking about. "Is it my birthday?"

"No, doofus. *Look.* 1785. They didn't officially declare it open until the next year, but they started planning the project, and moving the bones, in 1785. Which was also the last year Benjamin Franklin was in Paris."

"Whoa. You mean—"

"He hid something down there."

It got so quiet Dan could hear roaches scuttling in the closet.

"So," Nellie said, "we have to go underground, into a maze filled with bones, and find . . . whatever it is."

Amy nodded. "Except the Catacombs are huge. We don't know where to look. The only thing I can think— there's one public entrance. It says here it's across from the Denfert-Rochereau Métro station, in the 14th arrondissement."

"But if that's the only public entrance," Dan said, "then the other teams might head there, too. Everybody's been stealing that almanac from each other. They'll figure out the Maze of Bones thing eventually, if they haven't already."

"Good enough for me." Nellie brushed the chocolate and bread crumbs off her shirt. "Let's go meet your family."

Dan's backpack was a lot lighter today, but before they left he made sure the photo of his parents was still safe in the side pocket. His mom and dad were right where he'd left them: in their plastic photo album sheet, smiling from the top of their mountain like they hadn't minded sharing space with a Franklin battery and a grenade at all.

He wondered if they'd be proud of him for getting out of that pit last night, or if they'd be all protective like Amy: *You almost got yourself killed,* blah, blah, blah. He decided they would've been cooler than that. They'd probably had tons of dangerous adventures. Maybe *their* house had an arsenal, too, before it burned down.

"Dan!" Amy called. "Get out of the bathroom and let's go!"

"Coming!" he shouted. He looked at his parents one more time. "Thanks for the note about the Maze of Bones, Mom. I won't let you down!"

He slipped the photo back into his pack and went to join Amy and Nellie.

They weren't out of the Denfert-Rochereau Métro station two minutes before they spotted Uncle Alistair. He was kind of hard to miss in his cherry-red suit and canary-yellow ascot, his diamond-tipped cane swinging in one hand. The old man sauntered toward them, smiling with his arms out. As he got closer, Dan noticed he had a black eye.

"My dear children!"

Nellie whopped him upside the head with her backpack.

"Ow!" Uncle Alistair curled over, cupping his hand over his good eye.

"Nellie!" Amy said.

"Sorry," Nellie muttered. "I thought he was one of the bad guys."

"He is," Dan agreed.

"No, no." Alistair tried to smile, but all he could do was wince and blink. Dan figured his *other* eye was going to be black now thanks to that pop. Nellie's backpack was not light. "Children, please, you must believe me, I am *not* your enemy!"

"You stole the book from us," Dan said, "and left us for dead!"

"Children, I admit it. I thought you were lost in the fire. I barely made it out myself. Fortunately, I found a latch that opened the door. I called for you, but you must have discovered another way out. I had the almanac, yes. I couldn't leave it behind. I admit I panicked when I got outside. I feared our enemies were still about, or that I would be blamed for the terrible fire. So I fled. Forgive me."

Amy's scowl softened, but Dan didn't believe this guy at all.

"He's lying!" Dan said. "'Trust no one,' remember?"

"Should I hit him again?" Nellie asked.

Uncle Alistair flinched. "Please, listen. The Catacombs are right there." He pointed across the street to a simple building with a black facade. White letters above the door read ENTRÉE DES CATACOMBES.

The street around it looked like a normal neighborhood—townhouses, apartments, pedestrians on their way to work. It was hard to believe a maze of dead people lay right underneath.

"I must speak with you before you go in," Alistair insisted. "All I ask is ten minutes. You are in grave danger."

"*Grave* danger," Dan grumbled. "That supposed to be a joke?"

"Dan . . ." Amy put her hand on his arm. "Maybe we should listen to him. Ten minutes. What do we have to lose?"

Dan could think of a lot of things, but Alistair smiled.

"Thank you, my dear. There is a café just here. Shall we?"

Alistair was buying, so Dan ordered an early lunch— a turkey-and-cheese sandwich with chips and a large Coke, which for some weird reason was delivered in a glass with no ice. Nellie spoke with the waiter in French for a long time and ordered some exotic gourmet thing. The waiter looked impressed with her choice, but when it came Dan couldn't tell what it was. It looked like gobs of Silly Putty in garlic butter.

In a sad voice, Alistair explained how the Holts had ambushed him outside de Gaulle Airport and taken the *Poor Richard's Almanack*. "The barbarians hit me in the face and cracked one of my ribs. I really am getting too old for this sort of thing." He touched his bruised eyes.

"But . . . why is everyone trying to kill each other over that book?" Amy asked. "Aren't there other ways to find the clue? Like the invisible message we found in Philadelphia —"

"Amy!" Dan said. "Keep secrets much?"

"It's all right, my boy," Alistair said. "You're correct, of course, Amy. There are many possible paths toward the next clue. For instance, I found a message encoded in a famous portrait by — well, here, see for yourself."

Uncle Alistair reached into his coat and pulled out a paper. He unfolded a color print of a painting. It showed Benjamin Franklin as an old man in a red flowing robe, sitting in a thunderstorm, which seemed kind of dumb. A bunch of baby angels hovered around him — two at his feet, working on batteries, and three more right behind him, holding up a kite with a key on the string. Lightning zapped from the key into Ben's upraised hand. Ben didn't look upset by this. His long gray hair was wild and frizzed out, so maybe he was used to getting shocked.

"No way did it happen like that," Dan said. "With the angels and all."

"No, Dan," Alistair agreed. "It's symbolic. The painter, Benjamin West, meant to show Franklin as a hero for drawing lightning out of the sky. But there is more symbolism than I realized — signs hidden so deep only a Cahill could discover them. Look at Franklin's knee."

Dan didn't see anything except a knee, but Amy gasped. "That shape in the fabric!"

Dan squinted, and he saw what she meant. Part of Franklin's knee was painted in a lighter shade of red, but it wasn't just a random blotch. It was a silhouette he'd seen many times before.

"Whoa," he said. "The Lucian crest."

Nellie squinted. "That? That looks like one of those ladies on a trucker's mud flaps."

"No, it's two snakes around a sword," Amy said. "Trust me, if you'd seen the Lucian crest, you'd recognize it."

"There's more," Alistair said. "Look at the paper Franklin is holding. Turn it upside down. There—brushed over with white paint, almost impossible to read."

Dan never would've noticed if Alistair hadn't said something, but when he looked closely, he could see the faint shadow of words on the document in Franklin's hand.

"'Paris,'" he read. "'1785.'"

"Exactly, my dear boy: a painting of Franklin with a key, the Cahill family crest, and the words *Paris, 1785*. A significant hint."

"I never would've found this," Amy said in amazement.

Alistair shrugged. "As you said, my dear, there are many possible hints, all leading us along the path to the second clue. Unfortunately, we Cahills would rather fight each other, steal information, and keep each other from getting ahead"—he shifted his weight and winced—"as my cracked rib and black eyes will testify."

"But who buried all these hints in the first place?" Amy demanded. "Franklin?"

Alistair sipped his espresso. "I don't know, my dear. If I were to guess, I'd say it is a hodgepodge, a collected effort by many Cahills over the centuries. Dear old Grace seems to be the one who wove them all together, though why or how, I don't know. Whatever the final treasure is, the greatest Cahill minds have gone to a good deal of trouble to hide it. Or perhaps, as in the case of Benjamin Franklin, some of them are trying to lead us *toward* it. I suppose we will only know for certain when we find the treasure."

"We?" Dan said.

"I still believe we must have an alliance," Alistair said.

"Uh-uh." Nellie shook her head. "Don't trust this guy, kiddos. He's too smooth."

Alistair laughed. "And you're an expert on *smooth,* my teenage babysitter?"

"Au pair!" Nellie corrected.

Alistair looked like he wanted to make another joke at her expense. Then he glanced at her lethal backpack and apparently changed his mind.

"The point is, children, our competitors have decided *you* are the team to beat."

"But why us?" Amy demanded.

Alistair shrugged. "You've been ahead of the game so far. You have escaped every trap. You were always Grace's favorites." His eyes glittered, like a starving man looking at a Big Mac. "Let's be honest, eh? We all believe Grace gave you inside information. She must have. Tell me what it is, and I can help you."

Dan clenched his fists. He remembered that video of Grace, how stunned he'd felt when she'd announced the contest. Grace *should* have given them inside information. If she'd really loved them, she wouldn't have left them in the dark. The other teams were after them now because they thought Amy and Dan were Grace's favorites. But apparently Grace hadn't cared about them. They were just another team in this big cruel game she'd cooked up. The more he thought about it, the more betrayed he felt. He looked at the jade necklace around Amy's neck. He wanted to yank it off and throw it away. His eyes started to burn.

"We don't have inside information," he mumbled.

"Come now, my boy," Alistair said. "You *are* in danger. I could protect you. We could search the Catacombs together."

"We'll search by ourselves," Dan said.

"As you wish, my boy. But be aware: The Catacombs are huge. There are miles of tunnels. Most aren't even mapped. You can easily get lost down there. Special police patrol it to keep out trespassers. Some of the tunnels are flooded. Others collapse from time to time. Searching for Franklin's clue in the Catacombs will be dangerous and futile unless"— he leaned forward and raised his eyebrows —"unless you *do* know something you haven't told me. The almanac had a note in the margin. It mentioned coordinates in a box. You wouldn't happen to know what this box might be?"

"Even if we knew," Dan said, "we wouldn't tell you."

Amy touched the jade necklace at her collar. "Sorry, Uncle Alistair."

"I see." Alistair sat back. "I admire your spirit. But what if I were to . . . trade information? I'm sure you are wondering about those notes your mother made. I knew your parents. I could explain a few things."

Dan felt as if the air had turned to glass. He was afraid to move or he might get cut. "What few things?"

Alistair smiled, like he knew he'd hooked them. "Your mother's interest in the clues, perhaps. Or what your father really did for a living."

"He was a math professor," Amy said.

"Mmm." Alistair's smile was so irritating Dan was tempted to tell Nellie to whack him with the backpack again. "Maybe you'd like to know about the night they died?"

The turkey-and-cheese sandwich churned in Dan's stomach. "What do you know about that?"

"Many years ago, your mother—" Alistair stopped abruptly. His eyes fixed on something across the street. "Children, we must continue this later. I believe you *should* look in the Catacombs by yourselves. I'll stay behind, as a show of good faith."

"What do you mean?" Dan demanded.

Alistair pointed with his cane. A hundred yards down the street, Ian and Natalie Kabra were pushing through the crowd, hurrying toward the Catacombs entrance.

"I'll hold them off as long as I can," Alistair promised. "Now get underground quickly!"

CHAPTER 16

Amy hated crowds, but the idea of plunging into the middle of seven million dead people didn't bother her.

Nellie, Dan, and she hurried down a metal staircase. They found themselves in a limestone corridor with metal pipes running overhead and dim electric lights. The warm air smelled of mildew and wet rock.

"Only one exit, guys," Nellie said nervously. "If we get caught down here—"

"The tunnel should branch out soon," Amy said, trying to sound more confident than she felt.

The stone walls were etched with graffiti. Some looked recent, some ancient. One inscription was engraved on a marble slab right above their heads.

"*Stop, mortals,*" Nellie translated. "*This is the empire of death.*"

"Cheerful," Dan muttered.

They kept walking. The floor under Amy's feet was slushy gravel. Amy was still thinking about Uncle Alistair. Had he really known something about their parents, or was he just manipulating them? She tried to put it out of her mind.

"Where are the bones?" Dan asked. Then they turned a corner into a large room and Dan said, "Oh."

It was the creepiest place Amy had ever seen. Against the walls, human bones were stacked like firewood from the floor to above Amy's head. The remains were yellow and brown — mostly leg bones, but skulls stared out here and there like patches on a quilt. A line of skulls topped each stack.

Amy walked in awed silence. The next room was the same as the first — wall after wall of moldering remains. Dim electric lights cast eerie shadows over the dead, making their empty eye sockets look even scarier.

"Gross," Nellie managed. "There's, like, thousands."

"Millions," Amy said. "This is only one small part."

"They dug all these people up?" Dan asked. "Who would want that job?"

Amy didn't know, but she was amazed how the workers had made patterns with skulls in the stacks of femurs — diagonals, stripes, connect-the-dot shapes. In a weird, horrible way, it was almost beautiful.

In the third room, they found a stone altar with unlit candles.

"We need to find the oldest section," Amy said. "These bones are too recent. Look at the plaque. It's from 1804."

She led the way. Eyeless sockets of the dead seemed to stare at them as they passed.

"These are cool," Dan decided. "Maybe I could—"

"No, Dan," Amy said. "You can't collect human bones."

"Awww."

Nellie mumbled something that sounded like a prayer in Spanish. "Why would Benjamin Franklin want to come down here?"

"He was a scientist." Amy kept walking, reading the dates on the brass plaques. "He liked public works projects. This would've fascinated him."

"Millions of dead people," Nellie said. "Real fascinating."

They turned down a narrow corridor and found themselves facing a metal gate. Amy shook the bars. The gate creaked open like it hadn't been used in hundreds of years.

"Are you sure we should go down there?" Nellie asked.

Amy nodded. The dates were getting older. On the other hand, there were no metal pipes on the ceiling up ahead, which meant no electric lights.

"Anybody got a flashlight?" she asked.

"Yeah," Nellie said. "On my keychain."

She pulled out her keys and handed them to Amy. There was a little push-button pin light. Not much, but better than nothing. They kept going. After a hundred feet, they emerged in a small room with only one other exit.

Amy shone the flashlight on an old plaque framed in skulls. "1785! These have to be the first bones put down here."

The wall they were looking at was in bad shape. The bones were brown and crumbly, and some had scattered across the floor. The skulls along the top had been crushed, though the ones quilted into the wall looked fairly intact. They were done in a square pattern—nothing exciting.

"Search around," Amy said. "It has to be here."

Dan stuck his hands into some of the gaps in the bone wall. Nellie checked the top of the stack. Amy looked into the skulls' eye sockets with the flashlight, but she saw nothing.

"It's hopeless," she said at last. "If there was anything here, another team must've found it."

Dan scratched his head. Then he scratched a skull's head. "Why are they numbered?"

Amy wasn't in the mood for his games. "What numbers?"

"Here on the forehead." Dan tapped one of the skulls. "This guy was number three. Were they on a football team or something?"

Amy leaned in closer. Dan was right. The number was very faint, but scratched into the skull's forehead, like someone had carved it with a knife, was the Roman numeral III.

She examined the skull below it. XIX. A square pattern. Skulls with numbers. "Check them all. Quick!"

It didn't take long. There were sixteen skulls woven into the pile of bones, done in four rows and four columns. Three of the skulls didn't have numbers. The rest did. They looked like this:

A chill went down Amy's back. "Coordinates in a box. A magic box!"

"What?" Dan said. "What magic?"

"Dan, can you memorize these numbers and their placement?"

"I already have."

"We need to get out of here and find a map. This is the clue—well, the clue to the *real* clue, whatever Franklin was hiding."

"Wait a sec," Nellie said. "Franklin scratched numbers on skulls. Why?"

"It's a magic box," Amy said. "Franklin used to play with numbers when he got bored. Like when he was sitting in the Philadelphia Assembly and he didn't want to listen to the dull speeches, he would create magic boxes, number problems for himself. He would fill in the missing numbers. The sums had to match, horizontally and vertically."

Nellie scowled. "You're telling me Benjamin Franklin invented sudoku?"

"Well, yeah, in a way. And these—"

"Are coordinates," Dan supplied. "The missing sums show the location of the next clue."

Clapping echoed through the room. "Bravo."

Amy turned. Standing in the entrance were Ian and Natalie Kabra.

"I told you they could do it," Ian said to his sister.

"Oh, I suppose," Natalie conceded. Amy hated that even underground in a room full of bones, Natalie managed to look glamorous. She was wearing a black velour catsuit, so she looked eleven going on twenty-three. Her hair hung loose around her shoulders. The only part of her outfit that didn't match was the tiny silver dart gun in her hand. "Perhaps it wasn't *all* bad that Irina failed us."

"You!" Dan yelled. "You convinced Irina to set us up at the Île St-Louis. You almost got us buried in cement!"

"A shame it didn't work," Natalie said. "You would've made a fine welcome mat for the mausoleum."

"But—but why?" Amy stammered.

Ian smiled. "To put you out of commission, of course. And to give us extra time to find this place. We needed to make sure this wasn't some clever misdirection by our dear cousin Irina. I should've noticed the magic box earlier. Thanks for your help, Amy. Now, if you'll move aside, we'll just copy down those numbers and be off."

Amy took a shaky breath. "No."

Ian laughed. "Isn't she cute, Natalie? Acting like she has a choice."

"Yes." Natalie wrinkled her nose. "Cute."

Amy blushed. The Kabras always made her feel so awkward and stupid, but she couldn't let them get the clue. She snatched up a leg bone. "One move and I'll—I'll crush the skulls. You'll never get the numbers."

It didn't sound like a very convincing threat, even to her, but Ian paled. "Now let's not be stupid, Amy. I know how nervous you get, but we won't hurt you."

"Not at all," Natalie agreed. She pointed her dart gun at Amy's face. "I think poison six will be adequate. Nothing lethal. Just a deep, deep sleep. I'm sure someone will find you down here . . . someday."

A shadow loomed up behind the Kabras. Suddenly, Uncle Alistair charged into the room and knocked

Natalie to the ground. Her dart gun skittered away and Ian dove after it.

"Run!" Alistair yelled.

Amy didn't argue. She, Nellie, and Dan raced through the other exit, into the darkness — deeper into the Catacombs.

They ran for what seemed like hours, with nothing but the pin light to guide them. They turned down one corridor and found it blocked by a mound of rubble. They doubled back and followed another tunnel until it submerged completely in murky yellow water. Soon, Amy had no idea which direction they were heading.

"Alistair said there are police down here," she murmured. "I wish one would find us."

But they saw no one. The little flashlight started to dim.

"No," Amy said. "No, no, no!"

They forged ahead. Fifty feet, sixty feet, and their light went out completely.

Amy found Dan's hand and squeezed it tight.

"It's going to be fine, kiddos," Nellie said, but her voice was quavering. "We can't be lost down here forever."

Amy didn't see why not. The Catacombs went on for miles and had never been mapped completely. There was no reason anyone would come looking for them.

"We could shout for help," Dan said.

"It won't do any good," Amy said gloomily. "I'm sorry, guys. This is not how I wanted things to end."

"It's not the end!" Dan said. "We could follow one wall until we find another exit. We could—"

"Shhh!" Amy said.

"I'm just saying—"

"Dan, seriously! Be quiet! I thought I heard something."

The tunnel was silent except for the distant drip of water. Then Amy heard it again—a faint rumbling from somewhere in front of them.

"A train?" Nellie asked.

Amy's spirits lifted. "We must be near a Métro station. Come on!"

She shuffled forward with her hands outstretched. She shuddered as she touched a wall of bones, but she followed the corridor as it twisted to the right. Gradually, the rumbling sounds grew louder. Amy groped to the left. Her hand touched metal.

"A door!" she cried. "Dan, there's some kind of lock mechanism here. Come here and figure this out."

"Where?"

She found him in the dark and guided his hands to the lock. Within seconds, the hatch creaked open and they were blinded by electric light.

It took Amy a few moments to comprehend what she was seeing. The hatch was more like a window than a door—a square opening about five feet off the ground, just big enough to crawl through if they climbed up to it. They were eye level with the side of some railroad tracks — metal rails on wooden ties. And something brown and furry was scampering over the gravel bed.

Amy jumped. "A rat!"

The rodent regarded her, clearly unimpressed, then scurried on its way.

"It's a rail pit," Dan said. "We can climb out and—"

The light got brighter. The whole tunnel rumbled. Amy fell back and cupped her ears against the sound — like a herd of dinosaurs. A train blasted past in a blur of metal wheels. It sucked the air right out of their tunnel, pulling her clothes and hair toward the hatch. Then, just as suddenly, it was gone.

When she was sure her voice would work again, she said, "We can't go out there! We'll get killed!"

"Look," Dan said. "There's a service ladder about five feet down. We'll crawl up to the rails, run to the ladder, and climb to the platform. Easy!"

"That's not easy! What if another train comes?"

"We can time it," Nellie suggested. "I've got a clock on my iPod. . . ."

She pulled it out of her pocket, but she'd hardly pressed the wheel before another train roared by.

Nellie's glittery eye shadow made her face look ghostly in the dim light. "That was less than five minutes. The rails must be for express trains. We'll have to hurry."

"Right!" Dan said, and just like that he scrambled up and out of the hatch.

"Dan!" Amy shouted.

He turned, crouching on the tracks. "Come on!"

In a daze, Amy let Nellie give her a boost. With Dan's help, she crawled out. "Now help me with Nellie!" Dan said. "But watch the third rail."

Amy stiffened. Two feet away was the black electric rail that ran the trains. She knew enough about subways to understand that one touch would be worse than a thousand Franklin batteries. She helped Nellie out of the hatch, but it was a tight squeeze. They lost time. The rails hissed and clicked beneath them.

"I'm okay!" Nellie said, brushing off her clothes. "Let's get to the ladder."

Dan started to follow, but he lurched when he tried to stand, like he was caught on something.

"Dan?" Amy said.

"It's my backpack," he said. "It's wedged . . ."

He tugged at it helplessly. Somehow, one strap had gotten looped around a metal rail, and the rail had shifted, clamping the pack into place.

"Leave it!" Amy cried.

Nellie was already at the ladder, yelling at them to hurry. Passengers on the platform were starting to notice them, too. They were yelling in alarm, shouting in French.

Dan slipped the backpack off his shoulder, but it was still stuck to the rail. He tugged at it and tried to open it, but he wasn't having any luck.

"Now!" Nellie yelled.

Amy could feel a faint rumbling in the tracks at her feet.

"Dan!" she pleaded. "It's not important!"

"I can get it. Just another second."

"Dan, *no*. It's just a backpack!"

"It won't open!"

The far end of the tunnel lit up. Nellie was right above them on the platform, reaching out her hand. A lot of other passengers were doing the same, imploring them to grab hold.

"Amy!" Nellie cried. "You first!"

She didn't want to, but maybe if she went first, Dan would see reason. She grabbed Nellie's hand and Nellie hauled her from the rail pit. Immediately, Amy turned and stuck her hand out to Dan.

"Dan, please!" she called. "Now!"

The train's headlight flashed into sight. Wind rushed through the tunnel. The ground trembled.

Dan gave the backpack another tug, but it wouldn't budge. He looked at the train, and Amy saw he was crying. She didn't understand why.

"Dan, take — MY — HAND!"

She leaned out as far as she could. The train barreled down on them. With a cry of anguish, Dan grabbed her hand, and with more strength than Amy knew she had, she yanked him out of the pit so hard they tumbled over each other.

The train rushed on. When the noise died, the passengers on the platform all broke loose at once—scolding them in French while Nellie tried to explain and apologize. Amy didn't care what they were saying. She held her brother, who was crying harder than he had since he was little.

She looked over the edge of the pit, but the backpack was gone, swept away into the tunnels by the force of the train. They sat for a long time while Dan shivered and wiped his eyes. Eventually, the passengers lost interest in them. They drifted away or stepped onto other trains and disappeared. No police came. Pretty soon it was just Nellie, Amy, and Dan, sitting in a corner of the platform like a homeless family.

"Dan," Amy said gently. "What was in there? What did you have in the backpack?"

He sniffled and rubbed his nose. "Nothing."

It was the worst lie Amy had ever heard. Usually, she could tell what he was thinking just by looking at his face, but he was hiding his thoughts from her. She could only tell that he was miserable.

"Forget it," he said. "We don't have time."

"Are you sure—"

"I said forget it! We need to figure out that number box before the Kabras, don't we?"

She didn't like it, but he was right. Besides, something told her that if they stayed here much longer, the police would come and start asking questions. She took one last look at the rail pit where Dan had almost died and the dark hatch that led into the Catacombs. Fear still coursed through her body, but they'd been through too much to give up now.

"Let's go, then," she said. "We've got a clue to find."

Outside it had started to rain.

By the time they found a café, Dan seemed back to normal—or at least they'd come to a silent agreement that they would *act* like everything was normal. They sat under the awning to dry off while Nellie ordered food. Amy didn't think she could eat, but she was hungrier than she'd realized. It was five in the afternoon. They'd been in the Catacombs a long time.

She shuddered as she thought about Ian and Natalie and the poison dart gun. She hoped Uncle Alistair was all right. She still didn't trust him, but there was no denying he'd saved them in the Catacombs. She had terrible thoughts of the old man lying alone and unconscious in the maze.

As they ate brie-and-mushroom sandwiches, Dan drew skulls and Roman numerals on a napkin.

"Twelve, five, fourteen," he said. "Those are the missing numbers."

Amy didn't bother checking his math. He never messed up on number problems.

"Maybe it's an address and an arrondissement," she said.

Nellie wiped off her iPod. "Wouldn't the address have changed in two hundred years?"

Amy got a hollow feeling in her gut. Nellie was probably right. Paris might not have had the arrondissement system when Franklin lived here. And street addresses definitely would've changed — in which case Franklin's clue was no good anymore. Would Grace have sent them on a search that couldn't be finished?

Why not? a resentful voice said inside of her. *Grace didn't care enough to tell you about the quest in person. If Dan had died in that rail pit, it would've been Grace's fault.*

No, she decided. That wasn't true. Grace must've had a reason. The numbers must refer to something else. Amy could only think of one way to find out — the same thing she did whenever she had an unsolvable problem. "We need to find a library."

Nellie talked to the waiter in French, and he seemed to understand what they wanted.

"Pas de problème," he said.

He drew a map on a fresh napkin and scribbled the name of a Métro station: *École Militaire.*

"We have to hurry," Nellie said. "He says the library closes at six."

Half an hour later, soggy and still smelling like the Catacombs, they arrived at the American Library in Paris.

"Perfect," Amy said. The old building had black metal security bars over the doorway, but they were open. Peering inside, Amy saw stacks of books and plenty of comfortable places to read.

"Why should these guys help us?" Dan asked. "I mean, we don't have a library card or anything."

But Amy was already climbing the steps. For the first time in days, she felt absolutely confident. This was *her* world. She knew what to do.

The librarians came to their aid like soldiers responding to a battle cry. Amy told them she was researching Benjamin Franklin, and within minutes Amy, Dan, and Nellie were sitting at a table in a conference room, examining reproductions of Franklin documents—some so rare, the librarians told her, the only copies existed in Paris.

"Yeah, here's a rare grocery list," Dan muttered. "Wow."

He was about to toss it aside when Amy grabbed his wrist.

"Dan, you never know what's important. Back then there weren't many stores. If you wanted to buy something, you had to send the merchant an order and have your stuff shipped. What did Franklin buy?"

Dan sighed. "'Please to send the following: 3—*Treatise on Cyder Making* by Cave; 2—*Nelson on the Government of Children,* 8 vol., by Dodsley; 1 Qty.—Iron Solute; *Letters from a Russian Officer*—'"

"Hold it," Amy said. "'Iron Solute.' Where have I heard that before?"

"It was on that other list," Dan said without hesitation, "in one of the letters we saw in Philadelphia."

Amy frowned. "But iron solute isn't a book. This whole list is books except for that."

"What's iron solute, anyway?" Dan asked.

"Oh, guys, I know this!" Nellie chimed in. She held up her hands and closed her eyes like she was remembering the answer for a test. "It's like a chemical solution, right? They use it for metalworking and printing and a bunch of other stuff."

Amy stared at her. "How did you know that?"

"Hey, I took chemistry last semester. I remember 'cause the professor was talking about, like, how they make high-end cooking equipment. Franklin probably used iron solute for his ink when he was a printer."

"That's great," Dan muttered. "Except for the fact that it's *completely unimportant*! Now can we get back to the magic box coordinates?"

Amy still felt something nagging in the back of her head, like she was missing a connection, but she rifled through the rest of the papers. Finally, she unfolded a huge yellowing document that turned out to be an old-fashioned map of Paris. Her eyes widened.

"This is it." Amy put her finger proudly over a spot on the map. "A church. St-Pierre de Montmartre. That's where we need to go."

"How can you be sure?" Nellie asked.

"The numbers form a grid, see?" She pointed to the margins. "This is an old surveyor's map by a couple of French scientists, Compte de Buffon and Thomas-François D'Alibard. I remember reading about them. They were the first to test Franklin's lightning rod theories. After they proved the rods worked, King Louis XVI ordered them to draw up a plan to outfit all the major buildings in Paris. That church was the fourteenth installation, at coordinates five by twelve. Franklin would've known about the work. He was really proud of how the French took to his ideas. That *has* to be it. I'll bet you a box of French chocolate we'll find an entrance to the Catacombs at the church."

Dan looked doubtful. Outside, the rain was really coming down. Thunder shook the windows of the library. "What if the Kabras get there first?"

"We have to make sure that doesn't happen," Amy said. "Come on!"

CHAPTER 17

Dan felt like one of the Catacomb skulls—hollowed out inside.

He was determined not to show it. He was embarrassed enough that he'd cried on the train platform. But he kept reaching for his backpack and it wasn't there. He couldn't stop thinking about his parents' picture, whisked away and lost in the Métro tunnels. Maybe it had been ripped to shreds, or maybe his parents would be smiling in the darkness forever with no company but the rats. All he'd wanted to do was make them proud. Now he didn't know if his parents would ever forgive him.

The rain was still coming down. Thunder boomed across the sky. Every few minutes a flash of lightning would illuminate the Paris skyline.

If Dan had been in a better mood, he would've wanted to explore Montmartre. It looked like a cool neighborhood. The whole area was one big hill, topped with a massive white-domed church that glowed in the rain.

"That's where we're going?" Dan asked.

Amy shook her head. "That's the Sacré-Coeur Basilica. The smaller church, St-Pierre, is just below it. You can't see it from here."

"Two churches right together?"

"Yeah."

"Why wouldn't Franklin choose the big fancy one?"

Amy shrugged. "Wasn't his style. He liked simple architecture. He would've thought it amusing to choose a small plain church in the shadow of a big fancy one."

That didn't make much sense to Dan, but he was too wet and tired to argue. They hiked up the narrow streets, passing nightclubs with music blaring and neon signs that gleamed against the wet pavement.

"I used to have a nightlife," Nellie sighed.

As they climbed toward the top of the hill, Amy told them what she knew about the neighborhood — how famous artists used to live here like Picasso, Vincent van Gogh, and Salvador Dali.

Nellie pulled her raincoat tighter. "My mom told me another story — why it's called Montmartre, the Hill of the Martyr. She said Saint Denis was beheaded at the summit, right where we're going."

That didn't sound like a very good omen. Dan wondered if they still kept the head in the church, and whether saints' heads really had haloes.

A few minutes later they stood in a muddy graveyard, looking up at the dark silhouette of St-Pierre de Montmartre. The church was probably taller than it seemed, but with the white basilica towering on the hill behind it, St-Pierre looked short. It was made of gray stone slabs. A single square bell tower rose from the left-hand side, topped with a lightning rod and cross. Dan thought the building looked angry and resentful. If churches could frown, this one would.

"How do we know where to look?" he asked.

"Inside the sanctuary?" Nellie asked hopefully. "At least we'd be out of the rain."

BOOM! Thunder rolled across the rooftops. Lightning flashed, and in that second, Dan saw something.

"There," he said. "That tombstone."

"Dan," Amy complained, "this is no time for your collection!"

But he ran to a marble marker. If he hadn't been a tombstone admirer, he never would've noticed it. There were no dates. No name. At first, Dan thought the figure carved at the top was an angel, but the shape was wrong. It was weathered and worn, but he could still tell—

"Entwined serpents," Amy gasped. "The Lucian crest. And there—"

She knelt and traced an arrow carved at the base of the marker—an arrow pointing down into the earth.

Amy and Dan looked at each other and nodded.

"Oh, you're kidding," Nellie said. "You're not really going to—"

"Dig up a grave," Dan said.

They found a toolshed around the side of the church. They borrowed a shovel, a couple of gardening spades, and a flashlight that actually worked. Soon they were back at the graveside, digging in the mud. The rain made it hard going. In no time, they were completely filthy. It reminded Dan of the good old days when Amy and he were young. They used to have mud battles and their au pair would shriek in horror and make them spend the evening in a bubble bath, getting cleaned up.

Dan didn't think Nellie was going to make them a bubble bath tonight.

Slowly, the hole got deeper. It kept filling with water, but finally Dan's shovel struck stone. He scraped away the mud and found a marble slab about four feet long by three feet wide.

"Too small for a coffin," Amy said.

"Unless it's for a kid," Dan said. "I could fit in there."

"Don't say that!"

Dan wiped the mud off his face, which just made it muddier. "Only one way to find out." He worked the spade under the edge of the slab until he found a crack and then started to pry. "I need help."

Amy joined him. Nellie got the shovel into the crack and together they heaved the slab aside. Beneath was a square hole, but it wasn't a grave. Stairs led down, into the darkness of the Catacombs.

As soon as they reached the bottom, Dan swept the flashlight around the room. It was a square chamber hewn from limestone, with a tunnel exiting to the left and the right. There were no stacks of bones, but the walls were painted with faded murals. In the center was an ornately carved stone pedestal about three feet high. On the top sat a porcelain vase.

"Don't touch it!" Amy said. "It might be booby-trapped."

Dan edged closer to the vase. "It's decorated with little Franklins."

He could make out Ben holding a kite in a storm, Ben in a fur cap, Ben waving a cane over the ocean like he was doing some kind of magic trick.

"It's a souvenir vase," Amy said. "The kind they made in the 1700s to celebrate Franklin's arrival in Paris."

"Twenty bucks says something's inside," Dan offered.

"No bet," Amy said.

"Guys," Nellie said. "Look at this."

She was standing at the back wall. Dan came over and shone the light on the mural. The colors were faded, but Dan could make out four figures: two men and two women, dressed in old-fashioned clothes — even older than from Franklin's time, like from the Middle Ages or the Renaissance or something.

Each was painted larger than life. On the far left was a thin, cruel-looking man with dark hair. He held a dagger that was almost hidden in his sleeve. Faded black letters at his feet read L. CAHILL. Next to him stood a young lady with short blond hair and intelligent eyes. She held an old-fashioned mechanism with bronze gears—like a navigation instrument or a clock. The inscription under the hem of her brown dress read K. CAHILL. To her right was a huge dude with a thick neck and bushy eyebrows. He had a sword at his side. His jaw and his fists were clenched, like he was getting ready to slam his head into a brick wall. The inscription read T. CAHILL. Finally, on the far right, was a woman in a gold dress. Her red hair was gathered in a braid over one shoulder. She held a small harp—like one of those Irish harps Dan had seen in the Saint Patrick's Day parade back home in Boston. Her inscription read J. CAHILL.

Dan got the strangest feeling all four were watching him. They seemed angry, like he'd just interrupted them in the middle of a fight . . . but that was stupid. How could he tell that just from a wall painting?

"Who are they?" Nellie asked.

Amy touched the figure of L. Cahill, the man with the knife. "L . . . for Lucian?"

"Yeah," Dan said. He wasn't sure how, but he knew immediately that Amy was right. It was like he could read the expressions of the painted figures, the way he could sometimes do with Amy. "Lucian branch. That guy was the first."

"And K. Cahill . . ." Amy moved to the lady with the mechanical device. "Maybe K stood for Katrina or Katherine? Like Ekaterina branch?"

"Maybe." Dan looked at the guy with the sword. "Then T for Tomas? Hey, he looks like the Holts."

The picture of T. Cahill seemed to glare at him. Dan could totally see him in a purple running suit. Then Dan turned his attention to the last picture—the lady with the harp. "And . . . J for Janus. You think her name was Jane?"

Amy nodded. "Could be. The first of the Janus. Look, she's got—"

"Jonah Wizard's eyes," Dan said. The resemblance was eerie.

"These four," Amy said. "They look almost like—"

"Brothers and sisters," Dan said. It wasn't just their similar features. It was their postures, their expressions. Dan had been in enough fights with Amy to recognize the look: These guys were siblings who'd spent years annoying each other. The way they were standing—like they knew each other intimately but were also trying really hard not to throttle each other.

"Something must've happened between them," Amy said. "Something . . ."

Her eyes widened. She moved to the middle of the mural and brushed away some cobwebs between K. and T. Cahill. There, small but clear on the painted horizon, was a burning house and a dark figure running away from it — someone shrouded in a black cloak.

"A fire." Amy clutched her jade necklace. "Like Grace's mansion. Like what happened to our parents. We haven't changed in all these centuries. We're still trying to destroy each other."

Dan ran his fingers across the mural. It made no sense that they could know who these people were, but he was sure Amy was right. He just knew it, somewhere inside. He was looking at four siblings — the beginnings of the Cahill branches. He studied their faces the way he used to do with his parents' photograph, wondering who he resembled most.

"But what happened?" Nellie said. "What was in that house?"

Dan turned toward the stone pedestal. "I don't know, but I'm thinking it's time to open that vase."

Dan volunteered. Amy and Nellie stood back as he slowly lifted the vase off the pedestal. No poison arrows flew out. No spikes shot from the ceiling and no snake pits opened up, which Dan found kind of disappointing.

He was about to open the lid when Amy said, "Wait."

She pointed to the base of the pedestal. Dan had noticed the carvings, but he hadn't realized exactly what they were.

"Is that . . . sheet music?" he asked.

Amy nodded.

Notes, lines, and stanzas were etched in the rock—a complicated song. It brought back bad memories of Dan's piano teacher, Mrs. Harsh, who'd quit giving him lessons last year after he painted her minor keys with Crazy Glue.

"What does it mean?" he asked.

"I don't know," Amy said. "Franklin liked music—"

"Probably just decoration," Dan said impatiently. Something was rattling around inside the vase, and he was itching to open it. He put his hand on the lid.

"Dan, no!" Amy said.

But he opened it. Nothing bad happened. Dan reached inside and pulled out a corked glass cylinder wrapped in paper.

"What is that?" Amy asked.

"Liquid," Dan said. "A vial of something."

He untied the paper and tossed it aside.

"Hey!" Amy said. "That could be important."

"It's just a wrapper."

She picked it up and unfolded it. She scanned whatever was on it and quickly tucked it in her shirt pocket. Dan didn't care about that. He was trying to decipher the words etched on the glass vial. Inside was a thick green liquid, like the slime he used to play with and throw at his friends. The inscription read:

Sa othu gearch sith, os I search ethe.
Sue yht slslki het urtht ot efre.

"What is *that*?" Nellie said.

"German?" Amy asked.

"Uh-uh," Nellie said. "That's no language I've ever seen."

Suddenly, Dan's whole body tingled. The letters started rearranging themselves in his head. "It's one of those word puzzles," he announced. "Where they scramble the letters."

"An anagram?" Amy said. "How can you tell?"

Dan couldn't explain. It just made *sense* to him, the same way numbers did, or locks, or baseball card stats. "Give me a piece of paper and a pen."

Amy fished around in her bag. The only paper she could find was a piece of crème cardstock — their original clue about Poor Richard — but Dan didn't care. He gave Amy the vial and took the paper. He turned it over and wrote on the back, unscrambling the anagram word by word:

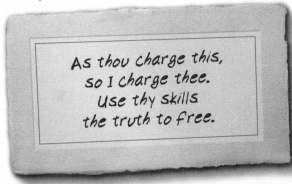

As thou charge this,
so I charge thee.
Use thy skills
the truth to free.

Nellie whistled. "Okay, I'm impressed."

"It's the second clue," Dan said. "The second *big* one. This has to be it."

Amy frowned doubtfully. "Maybe. But what does it mean—*As thou charge this*?"

Suddenly, light flooded the room.

"Good job, cuz!" At the foot of the stairs, dripping wet but looking quite pleased with himself, was Jonah Wizard. His father stood behind him with a video camera.

"Man, this'll make great TV." Jonah smiled wickedly. "This is the part where I swoop in, bust the lightweights, and gank the clue!"

CHAPTER 18

A rush of desperate energy filled Amy's body, like it had when she'd pulled Dan out of the rail pit. She hadn't come all this way to deal with a conceited jerk like Jonah Wizard. She imagined Grace's voice in her head, speaking with total confidence: *You will make me proud, Amy.*

She raised the vial. "Back off, Jonah, or . . . or I'll smash it!"

He laughed. "You wouldn't." But he sounded nervous.

"Awesome footage!" Jonah's dad said. "Keep it rolling, son. Great chemistry."

"And put down that camera!" Amy shouted.

Dan and Nellie stared at her in amazement, but Amy didn't care. She didn't care how valuable the vial might be, either. She'd had enough of the Cahill family's backstabbing. She was so angry she *did* feel like throwing the glass cylinder against the floor.

Apparently, Jonah sensed it, too. "All right, cuz. Take it easy. We're all friends here, right?"

"The camera!" Amy stepped forward like she was going to charge him.

Jonah flinched. "Dad, stop the camera."

"But, son—"

"Just do it!"

Reluctantly, Jonah's dad stopped filming.

"Okay, Amy." Jonah put on his dazzling smile. "We're good now, right? You know that's the second clue. If you destroy it, the whole quest ends. Nobody gets anything. That what you want?"

"Back up," she ordered, "into the corner. Go stand by Jane."

Jonah furrowed his eyebrows. "Who?"

"The mural. Go stand by the lady in the yellow—your great-great-great-great-great-grandmother."

Jonah clearly didn't know what she was talking about, but he went along. He and his dad backed into the corner.

Dan whistled. "Nice job, sis."

"Get up the stairs," she told him. "You too, Nellie. Hurry!"

As soon as they were up, Amy followed, but she knew Jonah and his dad wouldn't stay put for long.

"That was awesome!" Dan was bouncing up and down with excitement. "Can we seal them down there?"

"Dan, listen," she said. "The inscription *As thou charge this.* I think the stuff in this vial is inert."

"What's a nert?"

"Inert! Like inactive. It needs energy to catalyze it. Franklin messed around with chemistry. When he says a 'charge' . . ."

Dan grinned. "Of course!"

"It's dangerous."

"No choice."

"What are you guys talking—" Nellie glanced toward the street. "Oh, poop. Look!"

A purple ice cream truck was barreling toward them. It swerved to a stop in front of the gates. Eisenhower Holt scowled behind the wheel.

"Inside the church!" Amy said. "Quick!"

They raced up the path. Amy tugged open the sanctuary doors and crashed straight into a cherry-red suit.

"Hello, my dear children." Uncle Alistair smiled down at them. He looked like a raccoon with his two black eyes. Standing next to him was Irina Spasky.

Amy's heart crawled into her throat. "You . . . you and *her?*"

"Now, now," the old man said. "I saved your life in the Catacombs. I told you alliances are important. I'm simply making friends where I can. I suggest you hand over that vial, my dear. I would hate for Cousin Irina to use her persuasive techniques."

Irina extended her fingernails. A tiny needle sprouted from each one.

Amy turned to run, but her eyes widened. Something was hurtling toward her from the street—a large white cube.

"Duck!" she yelled. Nellie, Dan, and she hit the floor as a crate of ice cream sailed over their heads. The crate must've been from the back of the freezer, because it crashed into Alistair and Irina like a block of cement and knocked them both flat.

"Revenge time!" Eisenhower Holt yelled, pulling more frozen ammunition from the back of his van. Arnold the pit bull barked excitedly. The whole Holt family charged up the sidewalk, each holding a crate of crème glacée.

"Amy," Dan said nervously. "Are you . . ."

He didn't finish, but she knew what he was asking. The last time they'd encountered the Holts, Amy had panicked. This time she couldn't afford to. That Cahill mural in the secret room had steeled her willpower.

"Nellie, get out of here," she ordered. "They don't want you. Go call the police!"

"But—"

"That's the best way you can help us. Go!" Amy didn't wait for an answer. She and Dan dashed inside the church, leaping over the groaning forms of Alistair and Irina. They ran toward the back of the sanctuary.

Amy didn't have time to admire the church, but she felt like she'd plunged into the Middle Ages. Gray stone columns soared up to a vaulted ceiling. Endless rows of wooden pews faced the altar, and stained glass windows glinted in the dim light of prayer candles. Their footsteps echoed on the stone tiles.

"There!" Dan yelled. A door stood open on their left—a steep flight of stairs leading up. Amy latched the door behind them, but she knew it wouldn't hold the Holts for long.

They scrambled up the stairs. Dan started wheezing. Amy put her arm around him and half carried him.

Up, up, up. She hadn't realized the bell tower could be so high. Finally, she found a trapdoor and threw it open. Rain poured down on her face. They climbed into the belfry, which was open to the storm on all sides. A bronze bell the size of a file cabinet sat in one corner. It looked like it hadn't been rung in centuries.

"Help me!" Amy cried. She could hardly move the bell, but together, they managed to drag it on top of the trapdoor.

"That—should—hold," Dan wheezed. "Little—while."

Amy leaned out the side of the tower, into the rain and darkness. The graveyard looked impossibly far below. The cars on the street looked like the Matchbox toys Dan used to play with. Amy groped along the stone wall outside the window. Her fingers closed around a cold metal bar. A tiny set of rungs was embedded in the side of the tower, leading up to the steeple, about ten feet above her. If she fell . . .

"Stay here," she ordered Dan.

"No! Sis, you can't—"

"I have to. Here, take this." She gave him the paper that had been wrapped around the vial. "Keep that dry and hidden."

Dan stuffed it into his pants. "Sis . . ."

He looked terrified. Amy realized more than ever how alone they were in the world. All they had was each other.

She squeezed his shoulder. "I'll make it back, Dan. Don't worry."

BOOM! The bell shuddered as someone underneath, someone very strong, slammed into the trapdoor. *BOOM!*

Amy slipped the glass vial into her pocket and swung one leg out the window, into open darkness.

She could barely hang on. Rain stung her eyes. She didn't dare look down. She concentrated on the next rung of the ladder, and slowly, she pulled herself up onto the slanted tile roof.

Finally, she was at the peak. An old iron lightning rod pointed into the sky. At its base was a metal ring like a tiny basketball hoop, and below that a grounding wire, just like Franklin had recommended in his early experiments. Amy lashed the wire around her wrist, then took out the vial. It was so slippery she almost lost it. Carefully, she slipped it into the iron ring—a perfect fit.

She inched back down the roof. "Please," she thought, holding on tight to the rungs.

She didn't have to wait long. The hair stood up on the back of her neck. She smelled something like burning aluminum foil, and then, *CRACCCCK!*

The sky exploded. Sparks rained down all around her, hissing on the wet tiles. Dazed, she lost her balance and skittered down the roof. She grabbed frantically and caught a rung so hard pain shot up her wrist. But she held on and began to climb back to the top.

The glass vial was glowing. The green liquid inside was no longer murky and slimy. It seemed to be made of pure green light, trapped in glass. Carefully, Amy touched it. There was no shock. It wasn't even warm. She slipped the vial out of its brace and put it back in her pocket.

As thou charge this, so I charge thee.

The hardest part was still to come. She had to get away safely and figure out what she'd just created.

"Dan! I did it!" She climbed back into the bell tower, but her smile melted. Dan was lying on the floor, bound and gagged. Standing over him, in black combat fatigues, was Ian Kabra.

"Hello, cousin." Ian held out a plastic syringe. "I'll trade you."

"MMMM!" Dan struggled and tried to say something. *"MMMM! MMMM!"*

"Let—let him go!" Amy stammered. She was sure her face was bright red. She hated that she was stuttering again. Why did Ian Kabra turn her tongue to lead?

The bronze bell shuddered. The Holts were still pounding away below, trying to get through the trapdoor.

"You only have a few seconds before they come up," Ian warned. "Besides, your brother needs the antidote."

Amy's stomach clenched. "Wh-what have you done to him?"

"Nothing that can't be reversed if you act in the next minute or so." Ian dangled the antidote. "Give me Franklin's vial. It's a fair trade."

"MMM!" Dan shook his head violently, but Amy couldn't risk losing him. Nothing was worth that. Not a clue. Not a treasure. Nothing.

She held out the glowing green vial. Ian took it and she snatched the antidote out of his hand. She knelt next to Dan and started tugging at the gag in his mouth.

Ian chuckled. "Nice doing business with you, cousin."

"You'll—you'll never make it out of the tower. You're trapped up here the same as—"

Then something occurred to her. How had Ian gotten up here in the first place? She noticed straps running across his chest, like a climbing harness. At his feet lay a bundle of metal poles and black silk.

"Another thing Franklin loved." Ian picked up his bundle and began fastening the black silk to the metal frame. "Kites. He pulled himself across the Charles River with one, did you know?"

"You couldn't have—"

"Oh, yes I did." He pointed to the glowing dome of the larger church at the top of the hill. "I sailed right down from Sacré-Coeur. And now I'm going to sail right out again."

"You're a thief," Amy said.

Ian hooked his harness to the huge black kite. "Not a thief, Amy. A *Lucian,* the same as Benjamin Franklin. Whatever is in this vial, it belongs to the Lucians. I think old Ben would appreciate the irony of this!"

And just like that, Ian jumped out of the belfry. The wind took him. The kite must've been specially designed to support a human's weight, because Ian sailed smoothly down over the graveyard and fence and landed at a controlled run on the sidewalk.

Somewhere out in the storm, police sirens screamed. The bell shuddered as the Holt family pounded against the trapdoor.

"MMMM!"

"Dan!" Amy had completely forgotten him. She ripped off his gag.

"Ow!" he complained.

"Just hold still. I've got the antidote."

"Ian was bluffing!" Dan groaned. "I was trying to tell you. He didn't give me anything! I'm not poisoned."

"Are you sure?"

"Positive! That stuff he gave you is useless. Or maybe *it's* poison."

Disgusted with herself for being so stupid, Amy threw down the syringe. She untied Dan and helped him stand.

The bronze bell shuddered once more and lurched aside. The trapdoor burst open. Eisenhower Holt climbed into the belfry.

"You're too late," Dan told him. "Ian took it."

He pointed toward the street. A cab had just pulled up with Natalie Kabra in back. Ian climbed in and they took off through the streets of Montmartre.

Mr. Holt growled. "I'll make you both pay for this. I'll—"

Sirens wailed louder. The first police car appeared around the corner, blue lights flashing.

"Dad!" Reagan's voice called up from the stairs. "What's going on?"

A second police car appeared, racing toward the church.

"We're leaving," Eisenhower decided. He shouted down to his family: "Everybody, about face!" He took one last look at Amy and Dan. *"Next time . . ."*

He let the threat hang in the air and left Amy and Dan alone in the tower.

Amy looked out into the rain. She spotted Uncle Alistair hobbling away down a side street, a Fudgesicle stuck to the back of his cherry-red suit. Irina Spasky staggered out the front of the church, saw the police, and broke into a run.

"Arrêtez!" a policeman cried, and two of them started after her. Nellie was standing on the sidewalk with a few more officers. She was yelling frantically in French, pointing to the church.

Despite all the chaos, Amy felt strangely calm. Dan was alive. They'd survived the night. She'd done exactly what she needed to do. A smile crept over her face.

"Why are you so happy?" Dan complained. "We lost the second big clue. We've failed!"

"No," Amy said. "We haven't."

Dan stared at her. "Did that lightning fry your brain?"

"Dan, the vial wasn't the clue," she said. "That was just . . . well, I'm not sure what it was. A gift from Benjamin Franklin. Something to help in the search. But the real clue is that piece of paper you stuffed in your pants."

CHAPTER 19

Dan was thrilled that the second clue had been safely smuggled out of the church in his pants.

"So, really, I saved the day," he decided.

"Wait a minute," Amy said. "*I* climbed onto the roof in the middle of a thunderstorm."

"Yeah, but the clue was in *my* pants."

Amy rolled her eyes. "You're right, Dan. You are the real hero."

Nellie cracked a smile. "You both did pretty good, if you ask me."

They were sitting together at a café on the Champs-Élysées, watching the pedestrians and enjoying more *pain au chocolat*. It was the morning after the storm. The sky was blue. They'd already packed their bags and checked out of the Maison des Gardons. All things considered, Dan felt lucky.

He still had some doubts about what they'd gone through. In particular, he didn't like that Ian and Natalie had gotten away. He'd hated being tied up, and he wanted to get back at Ian. But it could've been worse. At least they hadn't gotten lost forever in the Catacombs or slammed in the face with a box of ice cream.

"I still want to know what was in that vial, though," he said.

Amy twirled her hair thoughtfully. "Whatever it is, it's supposed to give one team an advantage freeing the truth—that has to mean the final treasure of the contest. Since Ian and Natalie have the vial . . . well, I've got a bad feeling we'll find out what it does pretty quick."

"If these Lucian dudes created it," Nellie said, chewing on her croissant, "maybe it's like some special kind of poison. They seem to love poisons."

"Maybe," Dan said, though the answer felt wrong. He still didn't like the idea that Ben Franklin was related to Ian and Natalie. He'd started to admire Franklin—what with the fart essays and the lightning and all. Now he wasn't sure if old Ben was a good guy or a bad guy. "But what would poison have to do with a piece of sheet music?"

Amy took the parchment out of her backpack and spread it on the table. Dan had already studied it a dozen times. He knew it was an exact copy of the song they'd seen engraved on the stone pedestal in the secret room, but he didn't know why it was important. When he'd woken up that morning, Amy had already been researching on his laptop. Usually she didn't like the Internet. For some weird reason, she said books were better, so Dan knew she must've been really desperate for information.

"I found it online," Amy said.

"How?" Dan said.

"I did a search for Benjamin Franklin *plus* music. It came up right away. That's an adagio for armonica."

"Ben Franklin's instrument," Dan remembered. "The water on the glass rims thing."

"Yeah, but I have a feeling this is more than a musical score." Amy sat forward. Her eyes were bright, like she knew a secret. "We found the song and downloaded it. Listen."

Nellie handed over her iPod. "Not my kind of music. But whatever."

Dan listened. He felt like he was being filled with helium. The music was so familiar and beautiful it made him want to float across Paris, but it also confused him. Usually he had no trouble remembering things, but he could not recall where he'd heard this music before. "I know this song . . ."

"Dad used to play it," Amy said. "In his study, when he was working. He played it all the time."

Dan wanted to remember what Amy was talking about. He wanted to listen to the song over and over until he could *see* their dad in his study. But Nellie took back the iPod. "Sorry, kiddo. You've still got, like, mud in your ears."

"The notes are a code," Amy said. "The whole piece of music is some kind of message."

"And our parents knew about it," Dan said in amazement. "But what does it mean?"

"I don't know," Amy admitted. "But, Dan, you remember how Mr. McIntyre said the thirty-nine clues are pieces of a puzzle?"

"Yeah."

"I started thinking about that last night, after you decoded that message on the vial. I started wondering . . . why wasn't the *first* clue like that?"

She brought out the crème paper they'd paid two million dollars for. Dan's scrawled notes filled the back side. On the front side was their first clue:

RESOLUTION:
The fine print to guess,
Seek out Richard S_____.

Nellie frowned. "That led you to Franklin, right? Wasn't that the answer?"

"Only partly," Amy said. "It's also the first piece of the puzzle. It's a clue to an *actual thing.* That clicked for me last night when you mentioned anagrams, Dan."

He shook his head. "I don't get it."

She took out a pen and wrote RESOLUTION. "You asked me why this word was part of the clue. I didn't understand until now. We're supposed to guess the fine print." She passed the paper and pen to Dan. "Solve the anagram."

Dan stared at the letters. Suddenly, he felt like he'd been zapped by a Franklin battery. The letters rearranged themselves in his mind.

He picked up the pen and wrote: IRON SOLUTE

"I don't believe it," Nellie said. "This whole thing was about *iron solute?*"

"It's the first piece of the puzzle," Amy said. "It's an ingredient, or a component, or something like that."

"For what?" Dan asked.

Amy pursed her lips. "Iron solute could be used for chemistry, or metalworking, or even printing. There's no way to tell, yet. And we don't know how much we're supposed to use. Every time Franklin mentioned iron solute, he just wrote '1 quantity.'"

"We've got to find out!"

"We will," Amy promised. "And the sheet music . . ."

She spread her hands over the adagio score.

"It's an ingredient, too," Nellie guessed.

"I think so," Amy said. "That's how you can tell the *big* clues. They give you an actual ingredient. We just don't know how to read this one yet."

"But how do we find out?" Dan protested.

"The same way we did with Franklin. We find out about the person who wrote it. The composer was—" Amy stopped abruptly.

Coming down the street was a familiar figure—a thin balding man in a gray suit, carrying a cloth suitcase. "Mr. McIntyre!" Dan cried.

"Ah, there you are, children!" The old lawyer smiled. "May I?"

Amy quickly folded the first and second clues and put them away. Mr. McIntyre sat with them and ordered a coffee. He insisted on paying for their breakfast, which was okay by Dan, but Mr. McIntyre seemed nervous. His eyes were bloodshot. He kept glancing across the Champs-Élysées as if he was afraid he was being watched.

"I heard about last night," he said. "I'm so sorry."

"It's no big deal," Dan said.

"Indeed. I'm sure you'll be able to backtrack. But is it true? Did the Kabras really steal the second clue from under your noses?"

Dan got annoyed all over again. He wanted to brag about the sheet music they'd found and the iron solute thing, but Amy cut in.

"It's true," she said. "We have no idea where to go next."

"Alas." Mr. McIntyre sighed. "I fear you can't go home. Social Services are still on alert. Your aunt has hired a private detective to find you. And you cannot stay here. Paris is such an expensive city."

His eyes fixed on Amy's necklace. "My dear, I do have friends in the city. I know this would be a desperate measure, but I could possibly arrange a sale for your grandmother's—"

"No, thank you," Amy said. "We'll get by just fine."

"As you wish." Mr. McIntyre's tone made it clear he didn't believe her. "Well, if there's anything I can do. If you need advice—"

"Thanks, Mr. McIntyre," Dan said. "But we'll figure it out."

The old lawyer studied them both. "Very good. Very good. I fear there's one more thing I must ask of you."

He reached down for his cloth bag, and Dan noticed the claw marks on his hands.

"Whoa, what happened to you?"

The old man winced. "Yes, well . . ."

He plopped the bag on the table. Something inside said, *"Mrrrp!"*

"Saladin!" Amy and Dan cried together. Dan grabbed the bag and unzipped it. The big silver cat slinked out, looking indignant.

"I'm afraid we didn't get along." Mr. McIntyre rubbed his scarred hands. "He was *not* happy when you left him with me. He and I . . . well, he made his feelings quite clear that he wanted to be returned to you. It was quite a task getting him through customs, I don't mind telling you, but I really felt I had no choice. I hope you'll forgive me."

Dan couldn't help grinning. He hadn't realized just how much he'd missed the old cat. Somehow, having him here made up for losing the vial. It even made him feel a little better about losing his parents' photograph. With Saladin around, he felt like his family was complete. For the first time in days, he thought maybe, just maybe, Grace was still looking out for them. "He's got to come with us. He can be our attack cat!"

Saladin stared at him as if to say, *Show me some red snapper, kid, and I'll think about it.*

Dan expected Amy to argue, but she was smiling as much as he was. "You're right, Dan. Mr. McIntyre, thank you!"

"Yes, er, of course. Now if you'll excuse me, children. I wish you good hunting!"

He left a fifty-euro bill on the table and hurried out of the café, still looking around like he expected an ambush.

The waiter brought milk in a saucer and some fresh fish for Saladin. Nobody at the café seemed to think there was anything strange about sharing breakfast with an Egyptian Mau.

"You didn't tell Mr. McIntyre about the music," Nellie said. "I thought he was your friend."

"Mr. McIntyre told us to trust no one," Amy said.

"Yeah," Dan said. "And that includes him!"

Nellie crossed her arms. "Does that include me, too, kiddo? What about our agreement?"

Dan was stunned. He'd completely forgotten that Nellie had only promised to come with them on one trip. His heart sank. He'd started taking Nellie for granted. He wasn't sure what they would do without her.

"I . . . I trust you, Nellie," he said. "I don't want you to leave."

Nellie sipped her coffee. "But you're not going back to Boston. Which means if I go back, I'll get in huge trouble."

Dan hadn't thought of that, either. Amy stared guiltily at her breakfast.

Nellie inserted her earbuds. She watched a couple of college-age guys walking down the road. "This hasn't been a bad job, I guess — I mean, if I *have* to work with two annoying kids. Maybe we could make a different deal."

Dan shifted uncomfortably. "A different deal?"

"Someday when you find your treasure," Nellie said, "you can reimburse me. For now, I'll work for free. Because if you kiddos think I'd let you fly around the world and have fun without me, you're crazy."

Amy threw her arms around Nellie's neck.

Dan grinned. "Nellie, you're the best."

"I know that," she said. "C'mon, Amy, you're messing up my street cred."

"Sorry," Amy said, still grinning. She sat down again and brought out the music score. "Now, as I was saying —"

"Oh, right, the composer," Dan remembered.

Amy pointed at the bottom of the paper. "Look."

In the right-hand corner below the last stanza, Dan made out three scrawled letters in faded black ink:

$$\mathcal{W. A. M.}$$

"Wam," Dan said. "Wasn't that a band?"

"No, dummy! Those are initials. I told you some famous people made music for Benjamin Franklin's armonica. This guy was one of them. Toward the end of Franklin's life, he must've met this composer. I think they were *both* Cahills. They must've shared secrets. Anyway, I looked it up. This was the composer's last piece of chamber music. Its official name is KV 617."

"Catchy title," Nellie muttered.

"The thing is," Amy said, "there are lots of copies of this adagio. And there's still the version carved in stone on that pedestal. The other teams will figure out the clue eventually. We have to hurry and get to Vienna."

"Whoa, hold on," Dan said. "Vienna, Austria? Why there?"

Amy's eyes twinkled with excitement. "Because that's where Wolfgang Amadeus Mozart lived. And that's where we'll find the next clue."

CHAPTER 20

William McIntyre made his appointment just in time.

He stepped out onto the observation deck of the Eiffel Tower. The day after a heavy rain, the air was clean and fresh. Paris glistened below as if all its dark secrets had been washed away.

"They didn't trust you," the man in black said.

"No," William admitted.

His colleague smiled. "They learn quickly."

William McIntyre kept his annoyance in check. "Things could have gone worse."

"They could have gone much better. We will have to watch them more closely, don't you think?"

"Already taken care of." William McIntyre took out his cell phone. He showed his colleague the screen — the last number he had dialed in Vienna, Austria.

The man in black made a low whistle. "Are you sure that's wise?"

"No," William admitted. "But necessary. Next time, there can be no mistakes."

"No mistakes," the man in black agreed. And together, they watched the city of Paris spread out below them, ten million people completely unaware that the fate of the world hung in the balance.

TOP SECRET

Memo

To: The Cahill Family

If you are reading this, it means you are a long-lost member of the Cahill family – the most powerful family in the world. The source of the family's power has been lost and can only be recovered by assembling 39 Clues scattered around the globe.

Rumor has it that Amy and Dan Cahill have the best shot at finding all 39 Clues. But they haven't met their greatest competition . . . YOU!

Start Your Clue Hunt

1. Go to www.the39clues.com
2. Click on "Join Now" and choose a username and password.
3. Discover what branch of the Cahill family you belong to.
4. Explore the Cahill world and track down Clues.

Read the Books. Collect the Cards. Play the Gam

3 1901 05463 3112